# A MAN CALLED JESUS

THE LAND OF
# ISRAEL
IN THE TIME OF
JESUS CHRIST
30 A.D.

Sidon

Abila

ABILENE

Mt. Hermon

Tyre

Caesarea Philippi

Damascus

SYRIA

PHOENICIA

Raphana

Merom

Ptolemais

Capernaum

TETRARCHY OF PHILIP

Chorazin

Bethsaida Julias

Cana

Magdala

Gennesaret

Gergesa

Mt. Carmel

Nazareth

Tiberias

Hippos

Dor

Gadara

Megiddo

Nain

Mt. Tabor

Caesarea

Scythopolis

Mediterranean Sea

S A M A R I A

Sebaste

Mt. Ebal

Dion

DECAPOLIS

Antipatris

Sychar

Mt. Gerizim

Alexandrium

Joppa

Jamnia

Jericho

Emmaus

Amman

Azotus

JERUSALEM

Ashkelon

Bethlehem

Bethany

Gaza

J U D E A

Medeba

Adora

Hebron

Beersheba

Arad

NABATEA

Arabah Valley

# A MAN CALLED JESUS

A Novel
Revised and Annotated

Rick Herrick

SUNSTONE
PRESS
SANTA FE

Sunstone books may be purchased for educational, business, or sales promotional use. For information please write: Special Markets Department, Sunstone Press, P.O. Box 2321, Santa Fe, New Mexico 87504-2321.

Book and cover design › R. Ahl
Printed on acid-free paper
∞
eBook 978-1-61139-622-5

Library of Congress Cataloging-in-Publication Data

Names: Herrick, Rick, author.
Title: A man called Jesus : a novel revised and annotated / by Rick Herrick.
Description: Santa Fe, New Mexico : Sunstone Press, [2020] | Includes author's comments and reader's guide. | Summary: "A recreation of the Christian story for the twenty-first century"-- Provided by publisher.
Identifiers: LCCN 2021005771 | ISBN 9781632933263 (paperback) | ISBN 9781611394955 (epub)
Subjects: LCSH: Jesus Christ--Fiction. | LCGFT: Fiction.
Classification: LCC PS3558.E748 M36 2020 | DDC 813/.54--dc23
LC record available at https://lccn.loc.gov/2021005771

**WWW.SUNSTONEPRESS.COM**
SUNSTONE PRESS / POST OFFICE BOX 2321 / SANTA FE, NM 87504-2321 /USA
(505) 988-4418 / FAX (505) 988-1025

## ACKNOWLEDGMENTS

The first century Jewish historian Josephus described Jesus as a teacher and doer of great deeds. These great deeds included several healings of people he encountered with disease. From reading the novel and the Explanatory Notes, you will learn how Jesus healed disease and the basic assumptions he made in practicing his craft.

Our son Ben is a medical doctor who heals patients by using different techniques and by making different assumptions. Despite these differences, Jesus and Ben share two important characteristics in common. They both exhibit a wealth of learning and a sense of compassion for their patients. Because Ben inspires me with his incredible work ethic, his skills as a surgeon, his compassion, and his many other achievements, I am proud to dedicate this book to him.

Earlier drafts of this book were greatly improved by the comments of three special friends. Carol and Stephen Humpherys each read the manuscript twice, Googled questions they had related to my research, and came up with some amazing insights into the workings of first century Palestine. Many thanks also go to Bob Coe. If the novel is clean with regard to grammatical errors and the arguments in the Explanatory Notes are clearly presented, it is because of his important help.

# Foreword

In describing Jesus for the first time in *A Man Called Jesus*, I set his height at five feet, six inches. That was hard for me to do. I imagine him so much taller. In fact, I see him as just like me or maybe more like a Hollywood icon at six feet, two inches with an athletic frame. History tells a different story, however. Five feet, six inches was the average height of a Palestinian male living in the first century.

Contemporary Christians invent a Jesus that meets their needs and supports their values. The gospel of Mark asserts that Jesus earned a living as a tekton (Mark 6:3), the Greek word for a person who works with his hands; ie, a carpenter, stonemason or blacksmith. Several years ago I read a book about the historical Jesus in which the author used this information from Mark to argue that Jesus was a builder, a solid member of the middle class. This author wanted a Jesus just like him. In point of fact, a tekton was at the bottom of the social ladder. Jesus was not like this author imagined. He was a first century Palestinian peasant.

Why was such a misguided assumption possible? For 250 years scholars have been studying the historical Jesus; and, to date, there is no consensus as to who he was. Some of the most prominent views include apocalyptic prophet, prophet of Israel's renewal, charismatic religious leader, social reformer, and cynic dissident.

The problem is that there is no credible historical evidence about him. When Rome destroyed Jerusalem and burned the city in 70 CE, eyewitnesses were slaughtered by advancing Roman soldiers and written stories about Jesus were lost. In addition, first century historians wrote about kings, military campaigns, and Temple intrigue in Jerusalem. They had no interest in a peasant from the tiny village of Nazareth. Finally, the four gospels in the New Testament are of little help. With the exception of the two legendary birth stories in Matthew and Luke, the gospels all begin at the start of Jesus's ministry when he was thirty or thereabouts. We know nothing about his first thirty years.

In light of this situation, what is a scholar to do? An honest one will tell you the only way to proceed is to start with an hypothesis of who Jesus was and then to search for any available evidence to support your hypothesis. There is no objective evidence available for a study in which you gather all the data first and see where it leads you.

I have adopted such an approach in writing this novel. My Jesus is a religious leader who is deeply infused with God's love. This love defines his life. He celebrates the goodness of life. His God is one who brings joy and is quick to forgive. Judgment and wrath are not about who this God is. This is the God that supports and nourishes my life, and I assume that God does not change, that the God who loved Jesus is the same God who loves me.

In the pages that follow, I take these assumptions and create a Christian story. Please remember that everyone must create their own story because there is no credible historical data to provide guidance. In proceeding through the novel, you will come across some jarring depictions of a Jesus who is foreign to your preconceived ideas of who he was. One woman in reading the first edition burned the book after reading the first three pages. I have included Explanatory Notes which defend the strange twists and turns the novel takes using the best New Testament scholarship that is available. Please read the explanation in the Explanatory Notes before you burn your book.

On another level, the book can be used as a tour guide through rural Galilee and Jerusalem in the first century. You will learn how peasants from Nazareth lived, the challenges they faced, and the many threats to their lives they had to endure. In addition, we spend considerable time on the Sea of Galilee and in the magnificent temple in Jerusalem.

Finally, a major focus of the novel is on the teachings of Jesus. The application of these teachings to real life situations in first century Palestine may help them come alive for you.

No matter how you respond to the events of the novel, I can guarantee that you will love my Jesus. As he touches your heart, some of the unfamiliar events I create for his life may begin to make some sense. So take the plunge, and please get back to me with your thoughts about the book. My email address is rherrick86@gmail.com.

Before beginning, three explanatory notes are necessary. I use footnotes that appear at the end of each chapter to explain historical events that may not be readily apparent to the reader. When dates need greater clarity, I use CE for common era which replaces AD and BCE for before the common era which replaces BC. Finally, biblical passages quoted in the novel are taken from the Jerusalem Bible.

## 1: THE WATERFALL

It was the tenth day of Sivan, a late spring morning made warm by the hot sun of a cloudless day. Jesus and Anna were standing beneath their favorite waterfall located in the foothills of Mount Tabor, an hour's walk to the southeast from Nazareth. As the chilly water cascaded down on them, Jesus wrapped his arms around the swollen belly of his petite wife.

What a way to celebrate sabbath, he thought. The best thing about this sacred place was they could make love and then instantly become clean. There was no need for a ritual bath with all of this cool, clear water around.[1] He smiled deeply as he felt the baby kicking inside Anna.

"This water is freezing, my precious one," Anna said as she gently removed Jesus's hands from her and stepped away from the waterfall. "I'm going to sit and warm myself on the big rock."

"Wrap yourself in the blanket. I'll be right there," Jesus replied as he applied soap to his long brown hair. He lingered under the falls. It doesn't get better than this he thought. He had just made awkward, wonderful love to his beautiful wife, and their child was due in the next few weeks.

And then a dark cloud swept over him. The tax collector would surely come this week, and he hoped they had enough money to satisfy Rome's seemingly insatiable appetite for Jewish wealth. Raising cash was his responsibility. He left Nazareth each morning early to make the hour long walk to Sepphoris where he chiseled rock for the Roman theater being constructed on the northern edge of the city overlooking the Beit Netofah valley. His daily wages[2] were stored in an earthenware jar to be used for payment of the hated land tax.

The only good thing about Rome he thought was that if you paid the tax they left you alone. The warm support of his family and friends helped to put the rapacious beast out of his mind. But he too was getting cold, and so he quickly finished washing his five-foot, six inch body and stepped from under the falls to join his wife. He marveled at her beauty as she sat on the rock—the long black hair, olive skin, the shinning black eyes, and firm breasts that were gaining in size as her pregnancy progressed. She was spreading out their lunch of bread, dried figs, and olives.

"Moses must have been deeply in love with Zipporah," Anna said with a sheepish grin as Jesus walked from the river and climbed up onto the bank.

"Why do you say that?" he said as he reached for the blanket to dry himself.

"Because making love is not a violation of sabbath Law. Moses made so many things difficult on sabbath day, but he didn't ruin our fun."

"Most Jews don't understand the reason for sabbath," Jesus said as he spread out the blanket to dry in the midday sun. "The point is to honor God."

"If passionate feelings inside me do that, we did a good job," she said as she smiled across at him and handed him an olive. He squeezed her hand and sat down beside her.

"That's how I see it, Sweetheart. If you need squash for the evening meal, you pick it. No one can honor God if they are hungry. If your neighbor all of a sudden has a leak in his roof, you help him fix the roof. The best way I know to honor God is to help your neighbor," he said as he reached across for some bread.

"You know so much about these things, my Jesus. You should become a scribe or even a priest."

"My family needs me working in Sepphoris. Our land is too precious to surrender to the Romans."

"But you can read and write.[3] I can't even imagine that. Benjosef trained you well."

"I especially enjoyed copying sacred texts. Working on legal documents was less fun. Unfortunately scribes do a lot of that."

"How long did you train with Benjosef?"

"I started working for him when I was ten. My father would drop me off at his shop on the Cardo every morning before looking for work as a day laborer."[4]

"Your father was a fine man, though I didn't know him well. I was a young girl when he died."

"One of the many sad things about his death was that I was no longer free to apprentice for Benjosef. My family needed me working to earn coins to pay our taxes."

"Maybe you can take our son to learn from a scribe when he comes of age."

"I have been thinking a lot about how wonderful that would be. But a daughter would be precious too—especially if she looks like you." And he took her in his arms and kissed her passionately.

"I just want a healthy child, and the sooner the better."

"It won't be long, my Anna," he said smiling across at her. "The only unfortunate thing about this birth is that it will be harder to get to this wonderful place with a child to take care of."

"We can certainly bring our child, but it will be a little more difficult to celebrate the sabbath in our own special way," she said grinning across at him. And then a different thought crossed her mind. "We must bring our children here, my Jesus. They must learn to love wildflowers. They will laugh, and giggle, and play in these clear waters. Our God is all about goodness and beauty and love," she said as she gently kissed him before raising herself and walking across the long flat rock to gather her clothes.

"Hey, why are you putting on your tunic? I haven't finished eating yet."

"You can take the remaining olives with you. I need to get home to help your mother with the evening meal."[5]

• • •

Anna loved Jesus's family—his mother, two sisters, and two brothers who were still living. It was the only family she had. They all lived in separate houses; two-room stone houses with flat roofs, and packed dirt floors, that were close together, arranged in a circular pattern with a shared courtyard.

The courtyard was an important center of her social life.

Naomi, the youngest sister, was her favorite, a lively twenty-two year old who had a special place in her heart for her brother Jesus. She was married to Aaron who, along with Jesus's brother Joses, took care of the family animals and the animals of several neighboring families.

"Anna, you have the nasty job of plucking the four chickens."

"We must be celebrating, Naomi."

"Mom insisted. It's been two years since she has had a grandchild, and this is your first."

"Who knows when my first will finally arrive," Anna said as she sat down to work on the chickens.

"We're all betting this week," Mary said with a grin as she entered the courtyard with a jug of water on her shoulder. Mary was in her late forties, thin, healthy, and one who still enjoyed physical labor. "Where were you and Jesus all day? We missed you. You must have left right after the morning meal."

"We did. We went to celebrate the sabbath at the waterfall. We wanted to get away one last time before the baby arrives."

"Oh, it's nice to be young and in love," Mary said as she placed the jug on the shared stone oven in the courtyard. "Lydia brought some clothes over for the baby. She said they were owed for all the work Joses and Aaron do tending their sheep."

"Aaron never thinks in terms of being owed," Naomi said.

"Jesus is like that too," Anna said. "I'll be sure to thank Lydia. That's really nice."

"This is the first meat we've had since celebrating the Feast of Weeks two weeks ago," Naomi said.[6]

"We must have a strong Anna," Mary said with a smile.

"You are my second mother," Anna said as she looked up from the chicken and smiled over at her mother-in-law.

"Your parents were really good people," Mary said as she pulled up a chair next to Anna. "Let me help you with these chickens. Naomi, you gave Anna the most difficult job."

"I don't mind. It's good to sit. What I do mind is that our child will have only one grandparent."

"You can thank Judas for that.[7] We don't need any more messiahs."

"How did you escape Rome's burning of Sepphoris?" Naomi asked as she placed a large pot of squash onto the stone oven.

"I really don't remember. I was a one year old at the time," Anna said. "I just know that my father was brutally murdered, and my mother was taken as a slave somewhere."

"Your uncle Bartimaeus brought you here," Mary said as she reached across the table and squeezed Anna's hand. "Joanna and Andrew were without children. They were happy to take you in."

"Joanna did tell me something like that. They were so good to me. The best parents one could have. I miss them terribly."

"Isn't Joanna still alive?" Naomi asked as she added several pieces of wood to the firebox of the oven. "I thought she went to Cana to live with her brother after Andrew died."

"She is in Cana, bless her heart. Jesus and I will certainly take the baby to meet her as soon as our little one is old enough to travel."

"Will you ladies need onions for the evening meal?" James asked as he entered the courtyard. James was the farmer in the family. He tilled the family fields.

"No," Naomi replied. "Not for this meal. I have several baking in the oven."

"Will you boys be attending synagogue after the evening meal?" Naomi asked.

"I hope you're not late getting home," Anna said as she looked up at her brother-in-law. "I have no interest in going. Sleep is already calling me."[8]

"We're meeting at Philip's house if you plan to go, Naomi. I have no idea what the Hazzan has in mind."[9]

"Men talk," Naomi said. "I really don't think you men know much about God. My God is about children, and flowers. Beautiful waterfalls on the edge of Mount Tabor," she continued as she winked across at Anna. "Butterflies in the summer, gentle falling snow when it gets cold."

"You are Jesus's sister, Naomi," Anna said with a warm smile as she looked up at her sister-in-law. "That is his God too." She looked forward to their evening meal together as an extended family. Jesus worked hard to make it fun. He always told her the best place to find God was at a common meal.

• • •

It was late in the evening when Jesus climbed up the wooden ladder to the roof of their house to join his wife in bed. He took off his sandals, and quietly drew the rough-hewn quilt over him. He sensed the warmth of his precious wife beside him. As he turned away from her and closed his eyes, he quickly learned that sleep was not for him—at least not quite yet.

"Do you think God is watching over us?" Anna asked quietly as she rolled toward him and placed her arm across his chest. "Joanna always told me God looked at us through the stars, that the stars were God's windows to watch us from heaven."

"Do you mean watch over us or spy on us?" Jesus asked as he turned to his back and placed his hand on her arm. "He certainly has a lot of windows to peer through tonight."

"She never answered that question."

"I can't think of God as spying on us. It does make sense to think of him as watching over us."

"That sounds good to me. I'm only asking because I didn't want to go to bed without hearing that you love me."

"I do love you, Sweetheart. So very much," and he turned toward her, took her in his arms, and kissed her passionately.

"Now I can go to bed," she said as she slowly disengaged herself from him.

"I'm surprised you're still awake."

"My mind was racing about the baby, and the awesome prospect of giving birth."

"I'm scared about the giving birth part."

"You needn't worry. God will watch over us as you just said."

"I hope so Anna. I really hope so."

"How was the meeting?" she asked after a brief pause. She wasn't quite ready to lose him to sleep.

"Routine. Much like the other night."

"What did you discuss this time?"

"Mostly the land tax. Everyone there was worried about having enough coins to pay it. James made a good point about the tax. He said Rome should tax God. God is the real owner of all this land, not us."

"I just hope we can pay it."

"I wouldn't worry, Sweetheart. We have plenty of coins in that jar."

"You work so hard to provide it."

"That's why women are so special. I work to pay our taxes, and you will soon labor to provide us with God's greatest gift."

"It's my honor as a woman to do just that."

"I love you Anna, and now we must pray." Jesus took her hand. "Yahweh, God of our father Abraham and my favorite prophet Isaiah. Protect my precious Anna in her time of labor. Watch over the members of my family, and help my brother James learn that all of your Law can be summarized with the commandment to love. Good night my precious princess."

"Why are you picking on James?"

"I'm not picking on him. James is my beloved brother—so righteous and knowledgeable in matters of the Law. I just think God might want him to laugh a little more. But it's bedtime Sweetheart." Jesus hugged her tightly, and then turned on his side and closed his eyes.

Notes:

1. Jewish law regarding purity declared a man and a woman unclean after performing sexual intercourse. One remedied the problem by taking a bath.
2. A day laborer was placed at the bottom rung of the social ladder.
3. The literacy rate in Palestine at the time of Jesus was 5%.
4. Sepphoris was an important administrative city in rural Galilee. It was located three miles from Nazareth. Cardo, the main paved street in the city, was 45 feet wide and the site of the city's most important shops.
5. Please read my explanation of a married Jesus in the Explanatory Notes.
6. The Feast of Weeks is one of the three great pilgrimage festivals in Jerusalem. It celebrates God's giving Israel the sacred Torah and the

covenant committing the people of Israel to serving their God. It takes place each year on the sixth day of Sivan (late May or early June).

7. Judas, son of the famous Galilean bandit Hezekiah, led a rebellion against Rome in Sepphoris in 4 BCE. After initial success, he declared himself to be the messiah. Rome soon counterattacked and burned the city to the ground, killing thousands of Jews in the attack.

8. Women were allowed to attend public meetings in rural Galilee at the time of Jesus. They were not allowed to attend similar events in Jerusalem. Upper class women were especially confined to their homes. See the discussion of the contrasting cultures between Galilee and Judea in the Explanatory Notes.

9. There was no established synagogue (a building) in Nazareth or within Galilee until the third century of the common era. Before that time Jews met in people's houses, a shared courtyard or at the village gate. The Hassan served as a master of ceremonies for these public events.

## 2: Into the Wilderness

As the cock crowed, Jesus quickly said his morning prayers, put on his brown tunic and sandals, and climbed down the ladder to the courtyard. He entered the main room of his house and sat down at the small wooden table where Anna had set aside a meal of bread, olives, and assorted figs. He poured himself a glass of goat's milk from the earthenware jug on the shelf above the table. After giving thanks, he consumed his breakfast with dispatch.

"Goodbye my precious Anna," he whispered up at the roof as he exited the door of his two-room house. He rapidly walked through the sleeping village to find his friend Alphaeus. Alphaeus was a burly chap, tall, powerfully built, with a rugged face and stubble beard. But looks can be deceiving Jesus often thought. Alphaeus was full of fun, a mischievous prankster with a belly laugh. They had made the three-mile walk together to Sepphoris for the last three years.

"Jesus, my man," Alphaeus called out as he rounded the corner by the community well. "May Yahweh be with you."

"Good morning, Alphie. How goes it with you?"

"Couldn't be better after a sabbath's rest. Yourself?"

"Fine, Alphie, fine," Jesus said as he stepped forward to embrace his childhood friend. "My Anna and I spent sabbath at the waterfall. By the looks of her, it won't be long before she makes me a proud father."

"It won't be long now," Alphaeus responded as the two men left their village heading northwest along mud packed footpaths that made their way up and down the gently sloping Galilean hills. "I might be walking alone tomorrow morning."

"It may be a little early for that, but it sure is getting exciting around our courtyard."

"You're way behind me my friend."

"I know. I married in my late twenties. Marriage is more than a contract—at least for me. I had to be in love. It helped that both our fathers had died. There were no negotiations between families. I just asked her."

"And she said yes. Silly girl. Now she's stuck with a dreamer." Alphie smiled as his mind wandered to a time when he and Jesus were young boys. The two were riding sheep in his grandfather's meadow when he got ahead of Jesus and then lost him. It took twenty minutes before he found him sitting by a tree alongside a fast-moving stream. "Jesus, my friend, what happened? Where is Jesse? He's my favorite ram."

"He seemed tired so I got off here by this stream."

"Where did Jesse go?"

"He must have wandered off over that hill," and Jesus pointed to his left.

"What have you been doing all this time?"

"Listening to the stream. It's playing beautiful music. Can you hear it?" I've never been able to hear his music, but I love my dreamer and I know Anna does too, Alphie said to himself as his mind returned to the narrow footpath taking them to Sepphoris.

"Filling your mind with beauty and goodness makes our work go faster."

"Can you repeat that, old buddy? My mind was on us riding sheep."

"Jesse was a good one," Jesus said with a smile. "I was just saying that filling your mind with beauty and goodness makes our work go faster."

"My work stinks. I'm tired of that theater. It's been two years now. We build their buildings and pay for them with our taxes. The only people who will use that place are rich Jews."

"Wealth is not a problem unless it directs one's focus away from God."

"You're dreaming again my friend. Those Jews we work for are greedy, overstuffed pigs. Not a one of them cares about God. They pay lip service to a God they make up."

"You've become quite the philosopher this morning, but I agree with you. Sepphoris is a different place from Nazareth."

"I hate cities," Alphaeus said. "All their fancy two-story houses, paved roads, and government buildings."

"Do you think the building program will change now that the capital has moved to Tiberias?"[1]

"Why should it. They pay nothing for our labor. One denarius a day is chicken turd. The building program will never run out of money at that low wage."

"You're full of sour grapes this morning, my friend."

"I know, Jesus, and I apologize for ruining what for you must be a very special time. I'm just worried about the land tax. We are also paying on that damn loan we had to take out two years ago so that we could plant our wheat crop. That drought almost ruined us."

"You and everyone else are worried about that tax. How are the coins in your money jar?"

"That's what I'm worried about. We may not have enough."

"I think we have plenty my friend. You can have all you need."

"It's like we're fishing again," he said as he slapped his companion on the back. "Remember when we were little boys fishing in the stream above my parents' house. You caught two fish, and I was skunked."

"I couldn't eat two fish."

"You gave me the biggest one. That's why I tell Rebecca I love dreamers."

"And what does your Rebecca say to that?"

"That's nice, Alphaeus, but please keep bringing home that denarius."

"A sound woman."

"I know. I just wish I could get her to your waterfall."

• • •

While Jesus and Alphaeus were chiseling away at the theater, Anna, Naomi, and Salome, the wife of Jesus's brother James, giggled hysterically. The three women were in bare feet stomping grapes in the community-owned wine press.

"My husband is so righteous he makes me sick," Salome said as she grabbed for another bucket of grapes. Though worn out from childbearing, Salome was a hard-working woman who was generous to a fault.

"He's such a good man, Salome. How can you say that?" Anna said as she marched in place stomping on grapes.

"Of course, he's a good man. He just needs to loosen up. My little Benjamin went fishing yesterday without telling his father. When he returned, James accused him of breaking sabbath Law."

"Did he catch any fish?" Naomi interjected.

"Unfortunately, not. He was crushed."

"Then he didn't do any work," Naomi replied with a wide grin. "Little Ben is safe."

"I wish James looked at it that way. I also wish he would trim that beard. It's getting so long he'll soon trip over it. You're lucky Anna. You married the son with the trim beard who spends a little time taking care of himself."

"Jesus's beard tickles me. I love it, but to get back to the sabbath. Jesus says the purpose of the sabbath is to honor God. Sometimes work can do that."

"And so the two of you went to the waterfall. Can you imagine James and me going there on sabbath? He'd find one of those six hundred plus Laws to ruin things."

"James is his father's son. Daddy was always telling us to obey the Law, even in its little details. James obviously got that message."

"Whose son is Joses?" Anna asked as she looked over at her sister-in-law and smiled.

"Joses is the prankster. I'm not sure where he came from. Oh, hi, Mom," Naomi said as she looked across at her mother entering the courtyard with two additional buckets of grapes. "Where are all these grapes coming from?"

"James has the kids picking them."

"Come dance with us, Mary," Anna said as she ceased stomping to catch her breath.

"Are you tired my child?" Mary asked as she placed the two buckets on the wooden table next to the press.

"No. Just catching my breath."

"She's trying to tell her little one that if he wants to sleep, he better come outside," Salome said with a grin.

"Well I better go back and help James. We'll have lots of wine to celebrate with."

"Come back soon, Momma. I'm liking the feel of these grapes," Naomi said with a laugh.

"Running with grapes sure does beat chasing after children," Salome said as she balanced herself between the two women.

"Speaking of children, Salome. How long did you breast feed yours?"

"About a year. Maybe a little longer."

"It sure is easier to nurse them than to try to get goat's milk down their little throats," Naomi chimed in.

"That's what I was thinking. About a year."

"Momma," a ten-year old Benjamin yelled out as he entered the courtyard. "I caught a big fish. Can we eat him for dinner?"

"Sounds good to me," Salome replied back with a smile. "You deserve a fish after all your efforts yesterday, but you'll have to clean him."

"No problem. Daddy said I can use his knife."

"You be careful with that knife, son." As Anna smiled over at Benjamin, she lost her concentration, slipped, and fell down hard on the wine press floor. She took Naomi and Salome with her. Both women fell on top of her with a thud. A sharp pain radiated down from her stomach.

"My baby, my baby," Anna cried out in agony.

"Are you alright, Anna?" Naomi said as she tried to untangle herself from Salome.

"My baby, my baby," Anna again cried out, fear replacing the sharp pain she had just experienced. Salome pushed hard on the wine press floor allowing Naomi to stand. She then righted herself, and called out to her son.

"Benjamin, run! Get your father and grandmother. Tell them it's an emergency."

"Can I take the fish with me?"

"No, son. Run. I'll see after the fish. Naomi, you get out of the press, and I'll try to get Anna back on her feet." Anna was sobbing on the wine press floor, the right side of her face covered in grapes. "Can you move your legs, Anna? Let's see if we can get you on your feet." Anna continued to sob. After trying to lift her on her own, she looked over at Naomi and said. "I better wait for James. This is getting scary."

It took James and Salome together to raise Anna to her feet. James was then able to lift her up the side of the press and hand her to Jacob, their neighbor who was working in the fields adjacent to those owned by James and his two brothers. Jacob then carried her to a sleeping mat in Mary's house.

"This is serious, James. Go and fetch Jesus." Mary then turned to her daughter and said: "Naomi, it's time for the midwife."

"I'll get her immediately."

• • •

When Jesus entered the courtyard two and a half hours later, the first sound he heard was Anna moaning. "Yahweh, God of our fathers and protector of our mothers, please spare my wife and our child. Please help us. Please, please, please," and he fell to his knees burying his face in his hands. James knelt down beside him. "Come with me Jesus. Let's take a walk."

"Can I see her, James? Can I see her?" James looked across at his mother who shook her head no.

"Mom said you must wait, Jesus. Let's go out for that walk." Jesus slowly rose to his feet and looked across the courtyard at his mother. He pleaded with her.

"Mom, I must see Anna. Whatever is wrong, it will help if I hold her hand."

"Ruth says no one can see her—at least not right now."

"What's the matter, Mom? I don't see why I can't see her."

"You heard about her terrible fall."

"Yes Mother, James told me on the way home."

"She is bleeding inside. Ruth is trying to deliver the baby, but so far it has not been possible."

"Am I going to lose her, Momma? She can't die. She must not die."

"It's in God's hands now, my son." Jesus fell to the ground on his knees, and buried his tortured face in his hands. After a suitable pause, James gently guided his brother to his feet and out of the courtyard. They headed east toward the Sea of Galilee and the grassy plains.

"We need to find Joses," James said. Jesus dutifully followed behind with head bowed, fighting back tears. James tried to engage him in conversation, but his efforts went for naught. As they crested a grassy knoll after a forty-five minute search, Joses came into view. He was gathering his flock for the trip home. It was the tenth hour.[2]

"Hey Joses, we need you here immediately," James yelled out to his brother. He began to run toward them, but he didn't get far before Jesus called out.

"James, it won't work. Thank you for trying, but it won't work. I must see my Anna." He left in a rush, sprinting down the grassy knoll and across the verdant plains to his home. As he entered the courtyard twenty minutes later, the look on his mother's face said it all.

"We lost her Jesus. I'm so, so sorry." Jesus stopped short, winced in agony, and fled into the wilderness.

Notes

1. Antipas, tetrarch of Galilee from 4 BCE to 39CE, moved the capital of Galilee from Sepphoris to Tiberias on the Sea of Galilee in 19 CE.
2. Four p.m. A general way to gage time in the novel is as follows: the third hour is morning, the sixth hour is noon, and the ninth hour is afternoon.

## 3: John the Baptist

He headed south. Why? There was no explanation. He just ran, and then he ran some more. His eyes were bleary with tears, his mind was numb with grief. As the sun was setting, he passed the gate for the village of Nain. This would have told him he was traveling south, but his mind was not engaged in a way to make that recognition. He just increased his speed at the gate so as to avoid the possibility of encountering another person.

Half an hour later he collapsed beside a stream, and the floodgates opened. He buried his face in his hands and cried for his Anna—so beautiful, so young, so unfair. Briefly, he cried for himself. What would he do now? How could he begin again with a new life? When answers failed to come, he drank deeply from the stream and wandered aimlessly into the night.

The temperature was cooling, but he did not notice. His tunic was fraying as he bounced off branches and stumbled through briers, but he did not notice. His right leg was bleeding, but he did not notice.

The emerging starry sky was different. He noticed. He looked up, stopped suddenly, and yelled out: "Yahweh, how could you? If the stars are your windows, you're a fraud. You did not watch over my Anna. You ignored my sweet, Law-abiding father in his time of need. Where is the justice in your world? Why do the evil win, and the kind and loving die? You don't care. You are far away, so far away," and his words drifted toward silence as the anger inside him dissipated. He collapsed again onto the lush, green grass that makes up the Galilean plains and sobbed.

Eventually he tried closing his eyes, but sleep wouldn't come. His mind was racing, creating pictures of Anna at the waterfall and then on the mat in his mother's house fighting to survive. "She was so beautiful, so good. Our children would have honored you Yahweh, but you never gave them a chance. Oh my Anna, I will never laugh with you again. I will never be able to complain about my work in Sepphoris. You listened so well, Sweetheart. I love you Anna. I will always love you. I will never forget you," and sleep finally came. He slept fitfully until the sun had fully risen on the horizon.

He stretched, sat up, and started walking again. The first thing he noticed was the long, narrow trail of dried blood that ran along his right leg. "I don't remember cutting myself," he said to himself; and then his focus abruptly shifted as he tried to figure out where he was. A more important question was where was he going. No answers to either question were readily available.

So he kept walking, without a direction or purpose in mind. Eventually he remembered that last night he had passed by Nain. With the sun over his left shoulder, he concluded he was walking south. So what? Maybe I should turn back, he thought. Maybe I should return home to bury my Anna. It's the Law. And then he sadly concluded it was too late. James and Joses would take care of that this morning. I would never make it back in time.

He continued walking with the sun over his left shoulder, and looked for food. He was hungry, very hungry. Despite signs of a small village to his right, he kept walking. He was still not ready to encounter another person.

When he spotted a large rock just off from the narrow footpath, he sat down alongside it. He was desperately tired and distraught. He buried his head in his hands in anguish. He thought about Anna's life. So filled with tragedy, so unfair. She had lost both of her parents to the Sepphoris rebellion. As the first and only child, she had no brothers or sisters. I was her only family, and now she is gone. Why can life be so unfair? Where is God in all of this? Is God really in control? Why do I keep asking these questions?

In contrast and in hopes of lifting his mood, he thought about his own life—so blessed until yesterday. He had loving parents. Yes, he had lost his father ten years ago, but his father had been his best friend. He had sacrificed needed family income so I could work with Benjosef. He was so gentle and loving, strict about the Law, but also quick to smile and laugh. He taught me about the God in Genesis where everything is good, not the God of Joshua who conquers the land and murders Gentiles. Jesus thought about how he felt most of the time— filled with God's love and the goodness of life.

So much of that comes from my mother he concluded with a deep sense of gratitude. She taught me to swim in the streams about Nazareth when I was a little boy. We chased after butterflies, watched deer graze in meadows, and she told me stories at night. When he thought about those stories, they were never scary or about bad people. God was good, life was good, and people, though sometimes quirky, were created in God's image. He never remembered his mother speaking ill of another person.

This love and goodness are real, and yet so was the tragedy in Anna's life. How can our two lives be reconciled or understood? They can't, he concluded. Life and God are both mysteries—too deep for me to understand. Will the love and goodness come back? Not any time soon he thought, and sadness flooded his consciousness. He buried his head in his hands once more, and cried for his Anna. He dozed off briefly.

When he awoke with the sun directly above him, he was surprised and somewhat relieved that his mood had shifted somewhat. For the time being at least, the sobbing and the anger were over. He thought about his future. How am I going to reconstruct my life without Anna? What's the purpose? How will I find meaning without her as a part of my life? How will I find love? His eyes flooded briefly, but he kept on walking.

I am heading south he remembered, and then he had an important insight. Jerusalem. Oh, Jerusalem. I am heading your way. You might just be the answer. I need to learn more about you Yahweh. You have destroyed my childhood notions. Maybe Anna was right. Maybe I should become a scribe. Maybe I could honor my Anna by teaching people about your ways, Yahweh. Oh, you fool. I am a fool. I know nothing about your ways. I concluded that this morning, he thought to himself, and tears of self-pity welled up inside him. Without my Anna to hold me, without children to laugh with and instruct in the Law, I can't go back to chiseling rock. I need purpose and meaning in my life.

As he approached a stream to his left, he walked over to it, drinking in the clear cool water with relish. He removed his tunic and immersed himself fully. It felt good, really good. He then stood still in the water waiting for a fish. It was a race between two numbing pains—hunger and the affect of the cool water on his legs. The pain in his legs won. There were no fish, and he wondered if he could keep down raw fish anyway. He stepped from the stream, put on his tunic, and continued his journey.

Later that afternoon a strange thought occurred to him. I must be in Samaria. I have certainly traveled far enough south to have left Galilee. What if I encounter a Samaritan?[1] I better avoid them, but there are mountains ahead. I wonder if that one in the distance is Mount Gerizim? It was an Important thought. Many years ago his father had told him about his first Passover trip to Jerusalem. He had rounded Mount Gerizim on the left.

The thought he was headed in the right direction lifted his spirits. Those spirits soared when he came across an olive grove as dusk was approaching. He sat beside a tree and gorged himself on apple-sized olives. Refreshed with renewed energy, he continued his journey well into the night, stopping eventually to sleep under a dense canopy of trees on grass that was spongy with moss and dried leaves.

He awoke six hours later mad at God. Do you know I am suffering Yahweh? Do you care? Job was right. Your justice cannot be comprehended by mortals like me. Why is life so filled with sorrow? Is my Anna's death supposed to teach me a lesson? Never. You will never teach me that way Yahweh. I don't care about your justice. I question your power if you can't protect an innocent woman whose only wish was to honor you with the birth of our child. You make me sick Yahweh, and he burst into tears of guilt and fear. I'm sorry Yahweh. I hope your love can return to me soon. I need answers. And he arose quickly to continue his journey to Jerusalem.

Day three involved climbing upward as the terrain slowly gained altitude. He passed two shepherds at a distance and ran into several olive groves. The mountains came into clearer focus, which again buoyed his spirits.

Maybe I could improve my writing skills in Jerusalem, he thought. And then doubts flooded his awareness. The problem with being a scribe is that they do little teaching. Writing up legal contracts is boring work, and the contracts are often designed to keep the little guy poor or at a disadvantage. I guess I could specialize in writing scripture, but that has problems too. It meant working exclusively for wealthy people which is not who I am. Finding a purpose for my life without Anna is not going to be easy.

Thoughts like this filled his mind as he continued walking. As dusk approached, Jesus concluded he was tired of walking, hungry, and sick of olives. He was in the foothills of some mountain, and it was raining. Eventually he found shelter in another clump of trees within sight of a community well. The idea of a village nearby was somewhat disconcerting, but the trees provided cover, and he was too tired to continue searching. He curled up beside a tree and slept soundly for the first time in two days.

• • •

Rachel was an independent woman in her late twenties with a careworn face. She arose early each morning to go to the well in order to avoid contact with her neighbors. It was as if she had leprosy she thought as she walked along the path that led through the trees to the edge of the well. "Oh, my God," she said to herself in a tone of surprise and some anxiety. "It's a dead man." She approached the body gingerly and thought: should I touch him? Maybe he's not dead. Maybe I should turn him to see if he's alive. Maybe I should run to the village and report a dead man to the village elders.

As she stood there debating, Jesus stretched his legs and turned over on his side facing her. "Oh my. You are alive," she said.

"Yes I am, and who are you?"

"Rachel," she said. "I was on my way to get water from the well." Jesus smiled up at her, relieved and feeling good about the fact that he remembered how to smile.

"Jesus," he said. "My name is Jesus, and I'm on my way to Jerusalem. Am I in the vicinity of Mount Gerizim?"

"Gerizim is twenty miles further south. You have come to the village of Askar at the foot of Mount Ebal."

"Well at least I'm headed in the right direction," Jesus said as he lifted himself to his feet and brushed the leaves and debris from his tunic.

"From the looks of things you have had a rough trip my new-found friend. Your tunic is both tattered and torn, and your right leg looks as if it has been badly cut."

"It has been a difficult trip, but not because of some scrapes and bruises. I lost my wife in child birth three days ago and fled my village of Nazareth." And with that confession, Jesus burst into tears. Rachel moved toward him patting his shoulder and removing her shawl to wipe his tears.

"Woman, I am overwhelmed by your compassion. I am a Jew, and you wipe away my tears."

"Jesus, I am a woman who knows what it means to suffer. Let me fill my jug, and then you follow me back to my home in the woods. I can fill your belly there, and send you on your way with renewed energy and perhaps a new spirit."

Following a meal of baked trout, bread, and dried figs, Jesus did in fact feel renewed in body and spirit. "The only thing I love about my new life is I have learned how to fish," Rachel said as she cleared the wooden bowls from the table and placed them next to the jug of water. "It's such a peaceful way to spend time, and it keeps me full."

"Rachel, why are you living outside of the village?"

"Because I am divorced. I lost my house when my husband sent me that awful notice. All because I could not give him children."

"But why do you live separately from your neighbors?"

"Because the women of Askar see me as a threat."

"A threat?"

"I serve their husbands," and she burst into tears.

"Oh, Rachel, that's really sad. I have heard of similar situations. It's so unfair."

"That's the only way I can put meat on my table or get my roof fixed when it drips from the rain."

"Moses was a great man, but he made some mistakes. Divorce cannot be the will of God."

"It has certainly made a slave of me."

"God could never intend such a thing."

"Thank you, Jesus. Your voice is the voice of authority. Now you must move on toward Jerusalem."

"Can you give me directions?"

"Samaritans do not travel to Jerusalem, but I have talked with travelers who pass through here who do. They all head for Jericho. Travel east from here to the Jordan River. When you get to the river, follow it south. You can't miss Jericho if you do that."

"Do you have any idea regarding time or distance?"

"Not really because I have never been there. But my sense is Jericho is no more than a two or three day walk."

"You have done what you said you would do. I leave you with renewed strength and a lighter spirit."

"All the men in my life provide me with a brief stay. You are the first one whose stay has been brief but has filled me with respect. I will not forget you Jesus of Nazareth."

"Nor me, you. I will pass this way again when I return to my home."

"I look forward to that visit." Jesus instinctively moved forward to hug Rachel, and then he was gone. He walked along a narrow mountain path heading southeast for about two hours when he came upon a river that headed east. He decided to follow it, thinking it would eventually flow into the Jordan. It was a little scary because he came across no fellow travelers with whom to ask directions. He was somewhat surprised that his mind was relatively quiet after the last few days. His thoughts were mostly of Jerusalem and what he might see and learn there. He was glad that he was no longer condemning God, but there had been no easy answers to his questions.

Six hours after embarking on this gamble he was rewarded when the Jordan River appeared on his left. It must be the Jordan he concluded because of its size and the direction of its flow. It was a magnificent sight as the sun set on sparkling, clear water. He walked for another hour along the Jordan before stopping to bathe and to eat the bread, cheese, and fruit that Rachel had sent him with earlier that morning. He then walked up a gently sloping bank, found a soft spot of lush green grass beside a Sycamore tree and immediately fell into a deep sleep.

"Oh, my gosh. What is all that noise?" he said to himself as he rolled off his side, yawned, and squinted because of a sun that was already making the water sparkle from the opposite direction than that of last night. He sat up, adjusted his vision, and smiled as he watched eight men driving thirty-three fully loaded camels north in the direction of Galilee. He wondered what the camels were carrying and where they were going.

After the caravan was no longer in sight, he quickly got up, finished Rachel's provisions, and was on his way. The walk was an easy one, along level terrain and a well-traveled, mud packed road. It was a more interesting day because he had several brief conversations with travelers he met along the way. The conversations increased his excitement about what he would find in Jerusalem.

• • •

Jericho is the city where rich Jews play. It is also the city of palm trees and springs, located in the Jordan River valley six hundred feet below sea level. Because of its temperate climate, the winter palace of Herod the Great is located there.[2] The city also serves as a winter resort for much of the Judean aristocracy. Two days after leaving Rachel, Jesus of Nazareth found employment there.

As Jesus approached the northern edge of the city, he spotted a young man chopping wood in a cluster of trees not far from the stone-cobbled road he was traveling on. He approached the squat, muscular man and asked: "Kind sir, can you give me directions to Jerusalem?"

"Yes I can, but I wouldn't be starting the trip this late in the afternoon. The Jericho Road can be dangerous at night. Why not join my family for our evening meal. You can begin your travel in the morning."

"That's a nice offer you make. My name is Jesus," and he offered the man his hand.

"Nice to meet you Jesus. I am Thaddeus, the blacksmith."

"Let me help you with that wood. If your offer is a serious one, I would prefer to earn my supper. What can I do to help?"

"I need to transport this wood to my shop."

"Should I gather what you have chopped and place it in the wagon alongside the road?"

"That would be a great help. I'll lead you to the shop when it's full." On the way back from his shop, Thaddeus made an offer. "Do you have two weeks?"

"I have no definite date for arriving in Jerusalem."

"Work for me then. I can provide room and board, and some coins for your stay in Jerusalem."

"I guess I can do that."

"If you chop wood for me, I can start work on an iron gate for a wealthy Jew who lives on the other side of town.

"I could use a steady diet for the next two weeks," and he smiled across at his new-found friend as he separated from him and guided the small wagon to pick up a second load of wood.

• • •

Jesus enjoyed his two weeks with Thaddeus, his wife Hannah, and their four children. While he did not share with them the tragic events of the previous week, the warm, easygoing atmosphere of their home provided a bittersweet reminder of what he would be missing. The arduous physical labor involved with chopping and hauling wood was a great help in easing his sorrow. It focused his mind on the practical, and he was tired at night. He slept soundly in the crowded three-room house each night he was there.

His job with Thaddeus also opened up a unique opportunity. As they left the house early on the last day of his two-week commitment, Thaddeus said: "There will be no working this morning my good friend. We have been talking about John the Baptist ever since you got here, and we need to get you baptized. He usually baptizes on the Perea side,[3] but my friends tell me he'll be baptizing on the west bank of the Jordan River this morning. That's nothing more than a twenty-minute walk to the south."

"It will be good to be cleansed before my trip to Jerusalem."

"The point for John is to repent. Be ready with your sins."

"Oh, I have lots of those," Jesus said as they passed the blacksmith shop and headed toward the river.

"As I was saying to you the other night at dinner, he wants people to live righteously, to make a firm commitment to ethical living. We earn a place in God's glorious kingdom by doing good works, by being good Jews."

"I think God wants us to live that way," Jesus said.

"He's a prophet, Jesus. Some people think he is Elijah returned."

"Does he claim to be the hoped-for messiah?"

"No, but he says God's kingdom is imminent. We must repent or face God's harsh judgment. Sinners will burn. Being a Jew won't protect you."

"Does he mean the coming of God's kingdom will be a disaster for people who are sinners?"

"Yes. They will burn. It's really scary unless you repent and turn your life around."

"I don't know about that, Thaddeus. It troubled me when we discussed it the other night. We are all sinners. I can't conceive of a God achieving his purposes in such a mean-spirited way."

"You can decide for yourself, Jesus. We're almost there." Five minutes later as they climbed a small hill along the riverbank, a crowd of a hundred or more people came into view. "That's him, standing with his feet in the water."

"My, oh my. He's a strange looking man."

"He only wears skins from a camel. Come on. Hurry. I don't want to miss what he has to say."

"The time is at hand. You must repent and be baptized in this sacred river. Woe to you who thinks your inheritance from Abraham will save you from the coming judgment. Everyone who does not bear good fruit will be cut down. You will be consumed by fire. God is not mocked. So come with me, and let me baptize you in God's river. Repent with me, and you will be saved." With the conclusion of his brief remarks, John walked into the middle of the river.

"His message never varies. We got here just in time. Let's go, Jesus. I'm going to repent and be baptized for the third time." Thaddeus shoved Jesus forward. The two men entered the river, and waited their turn to be baptized by John. Twenty minutes later Jesus was filled with anxiety and dread.

"Go in peace, my son," John said to the man beside Jesus as the man emerged from the water. John then turned his attention to Jesus. He was tall and thin with a gaunt face, penetrating eyes, and a long beard. For a brief moment Jesus wished he was back in Sepphoris chiseling stone. "And who is this sinner before me?" John said without smiling, the intensity of his stare piercing a hole in Jesus's heart.

"Jesus of Nazareth, Master."

"Is this Jesus of Nazareth a sinner?"

"Yes, Master. I dishonored my mother by fleeing from her home three weeks ago."

"Do you repent of this sin, Jesus of Nazareth?"

"Yes, Master. I do."

"Will you turn your life toward God and live according to his commandments?"

"Yes, Master I will."

"Then I baptize you in the name of Yahweh, the God of our fathers, Abraham, Isaac, and Jacob;" and he placed his hands on Jesus's shoulders, thrusting him down into the water with considerable force. "Go in peace, my son," John repeated as Jesus came to the surface. John turned his attention to Thaddeus. All Jesus wanted to do was to escape, and so he left the water in a hurry.

"Do you feel cleansed, Jesus?" Thaddeus asked as the two men climbed back over the small hill for the short trip home.

"I don't know that cleansed is the right word for it," Jesus replied. "I'm just happy to be going back to work."

"He is a prophet, Jesus. Be careful what you say. Do not take his message lightly."

"There is nothing light about John the Baptist. I just wish he could have smiled at me. Listen Thaddeus. I don't want to belittle your prophet, but I have to admit to you I didn't like his God very much."

"What do you mean by that?"

"The God I heard coming from the mouth of John the Baptist is a scorching wind, a fiery furnace, a revenging tyrant. My God is more like a butterfly that gently caresses a flower, a father that forgives a disobedient child, a wife who opens her arms to receive her husband."

"You are a strange one, Jesus, but a very good worker."

"Thank you, Thaddeus. I hope your strange one is still your good friend."

"I can certainly agree with you on that." Fifteen minutes later as the two men entered the shop, Thaddeus said: "Now Jesus. Five more loads. That's it. Hannah is preparing a special meal to sustain you during the rest of your journey to Jerusalem."

Notes

1. In ancient Israel, the province of Samaria sat between Galilee to the north and Judea to the south. The inhabitants of Samaria were considered unclean foreigners because they accepted only the first five books of Jewish scripture, and because they worshipped Yahweh at Mount Gerizim, rejecting the temple at Jerusalem.

2. Herod the Great was the Roman client king of Judea from 37 BCE to 4 BCE. Jesus was believed to have been born in 4 BCE, the year of Herod's death.

3. The province of Perea was located on the east bank of the Jordan River just across from Jericho.

## 4: Jerusalem

Jesus ascended three thousand feet on the Jericho Road to Jerusalem. Three hours into this arduous journey, he came across an older man leading a donkey who was pulling a cart loaded with fruit. "How far am I from Jerusalem, kind sir?" Jesus asked with a smile.

"You couldn't be closer. In less than a mile, you'll arrive at the Mount of Olives which puts you on the southern edge of the city."

"Is it hard to find the Temple from there?"

"You'll take in the whole city from there. You can't miss the Temple. It's that huge white marble structure in the northeast corner of the city."

"Thank you so much. I'm excited to get there."

"Pray for me," the old man responded with a smile as he slapped his donkey on the side and was on his way. Ten minutes later the city of Jerusalem jumped out at him as the old man had promised. "Oh, my, it's magnificent. The view from up here is spectacular," he mumbled to himself. David and Solomon once roamed those streets as did Isaiah and Jeremiah. It's a great day to be a Jew.

His thoughts turned to the Temple. It dominates the entire northern half of the city. Even from this distance he could pick out three large ox driven wagons loaded with huge stones. They slowly rambled toward the Temple complex. The work continues he concluded. No wonder they keep taking our grain.

After taking it all in, he started to descend the steep slope that led to the city. It was an easy walk along a well-worn path with olive trees all around him. He soon ran across a stream where he washed his face and drank hungrily from the crystal clear water. In twenty minutes he arrived at the wall surrounding the city. Off to his left was a gate where a man with a cart loaded with vegetables was arguing with another man who was blocking the entrance into the city. This must be about taxes he thought. I'm lucky Thaddeus was such a generous employer. I have coins.

Jesus's luck continued as he walked around the merchant and entered the city without being taxed. A quarter of a mile into the city he saw a small sign which read Pool of Siloam. He entered the male section to take a ritual bath which was enormously refreshing after his arduous uphill travels in the hot sun.

The walk from the bath to the Temple went along a wide, stone paved thoroughfare with shops and small, densely packed stone houses on both sides of the street. Fifteen minutes later he climbed a wide staircase,[1] entered two gates that took him through a tunnel lined with candles and a carved, painted ceiling. He soon emerged into a large open space where several people were moving together in a counterclockwise direction.

He watched them circle an enormous walled-in structure, and as they passed by he noticed a man dressed in a military tunic with a sword at his side. He looks official Jesus thought and walked up to him. "Kind sir, will the Temple be holding a service today?"

"Yes. There's a worship service held there at the fourth and ninth hour each day. You are currently standing in the Court of Gentiles, which spans thirty-five acres. It circles the sanctuary. All visitors are allowed in this Court. You sound like a Galilean."

"I am. My native village is Nazareth."

"All Jews are allowed to observe the sacrifice from the Court of Women which you access from the gate over there," and he turned and pointed to the right. "Jewish men can get a better view from the Court of Israel. You can get directions inside for that."

"What's that huge tower just outside the wall off to the right?"

"That's the Roman fort of Antonia. Six hundred Roman soldiers are stationed there."

"Are you one of them?"

"No. I am a Temple Guard.[2] We are responsible for keeping order on these grounds. It may surprise you, but a lot of troublemakers come through here."

"I see. Well, thank you for your time. I may be back with further questions." When the Temple Guard failed to respond, Jesus smiled across at him and continued on his way. It wasn't long before he came across a puzzling and somewhat disturbing sight—animals corralled in circles, cattle and sheep, with pigeons in cages stacked high up on the ground. These must be animals for sacrifice, he concluded. There certainly are a lot of them.

Just beyond the animals there were tables where several people seemed to be exchanging coins. What's going on here Jesus wondered, and he returned to the Temple Guard. "Kind sir, what are the people doing at the tables?"

"Oh, it's you again. You Galileans come here with so many questions. They are purchasing animals to sacrifice. By the way, you pay your Temple tax there. Have you paid this year?"

"No. Not yet."

"Then you owe us half a shekel."

"I will pay on my way to the Women's Court." Jesus was happy to leave the Temple guard as he made his way to one of the many money-changing tables. He stopped in front of the first one he came to, went through his haversack, found the appropriate coin, and handed it to the nice looking man sitting at the table.

"Bless you my son, and please enjoy your stay in God's house." Jesus smiled back at the man before turning his attention to the man beside him who was arguing about the price of the lamb he intended to purchase for sacrifice. It dawned on Jesus while listening to this testy exchange that this sacrifice system was a business. There were other people haggling over prices to purchase innocent animals held hostage less than fifty yards away.

Do acts like this please Yahweh he wondered? What happens to all that meat? Maybe it would please Yahweh more if they gave the animals to the poor. You kill an innocent animal and like magic your sins are forgiven. I can't wait to talk to James about this.

As these thoughts were floating through his head, he began walking toward the gate to the Court of Women. Halfway there he ran into a group of men having an animated discussion. One was dressed in a long white robe with tassels. Jesus meandered over toward them. "What does

Caiaphas[3] do with all that money?" one man asked. "That half shekel takes some of us three days to earn."

"It goes to do God's work," the man in the white robe said. He must be a priest Jesus concluded.

"God must have a lot of work to do."

"Is it God's work to kill all those innocent animals?" Jesus asked from his position outside their circle. The five men turned to see who was asking the question.

"Those animals are sacrificed to honor Yahweh. Sinners sacrifice them to atone for their sins," the priest responded.

"Is Yahweh honored when the animals are purchased at a bazaar?"

"This is Yahweh's sacred Temple. He resides here. It's the Law of Moses. Yahweh requires us to atone for our sins with sacrifice. But you sound like you are from Galilee. Maybe Galileans do not know such things."

"Here is what I do know," Jesus responded to the priest. "The scribe I worked for in Sepphoris had me copy the book of Hosea. At one point the prophet loudly shouts: "I desire steadfast love, not sacrifice. Knowledge of God, not burnt offerings. Micah makes the same point when he says Yahweh wants justice and kindness not ritual practice."[4] The priest stomped off toward the sanctuary.

"Galileans are always causing problems," one of the four men said. He and his three companions moved toward the tables with the moneychangers. A tall, older man with long flowing gray hair and a gray beard stepped toward Jesus. He had a distinguished air about him which commanded respect.

"I like it when Galileans stir up trouble. My name is Lazarus."

"I am Jesus of Nazareth. Thank you for defending me."

"I never had the chance to defend you before the priest. He's nothing more than a stuffed shirt and a windbag."

"Is he employed by the Temple?"

"Yes. There are seven thousand of them. Many of them live outside of Jerusalem, but the ones who live here are the rich ones who live in palatial houses. That's what Amos the mason was getting at a few minutes ago with his complaints about the Temple tax. The priest you bested in argument has close ties to the Sadducees."

"Sadducees?"

"The Sadducees are a small group of upper-class Jews mainly connected with this Temple. They have some rather strange views,[5] but my main problem with them is they don't seem to be very interested in religion. They put on a good show, but their main concerns seem to be power and money."

"That's too bad; and they are priests?"

"They are not priests themselves, but they work closely with them. A priest inherits his position from his family. You can't aspire to be one. But I was interested in your comments on sacrifice. Let's go watch the service in the Court of Israel. That gives you the best view. Follow me."

As the two men headed for the Court of Israel, they continued their discussion. "You know, I never thought much about sacrifice until today," Jesus said. "It's not part of our worship in Nazareth."

"Here it's the main show," Lazarus responded.

"I gather that. It just struck me that the whole thing's a business. It also seems like a waste of precious food."

"I like what you said about justice and kindness. I've always felt that was more important than spending your savings on an animal to sacrifice. Now follow me up these marble steps, and we'll be where we need to be." They soon joined thirty or more male spectators.

"As you can see, it takes several priests to pull this off. There are five bringing logs for the fire, and three others are carrying the meat for the sacrifice. I'm not exactly sure where the actual slaughter of these animals takes place. It's not far from here, however. They have an elaborate system of drains to take the blood safely away. With thousands of animals slaughtered each year, you can imagine there is a lot of blood."

"Is all the meat placed on the fire?" Jesus asked his new friend in a whispered voice.

"No. Some is saved for the priests to eat, and the priests also take the hides which have considerable value."

"It's just hard to believe God wouldn't prefer these animals be given to the poor."

"I couldn't agree more. The whole practice is rather disgusting to me, but let me point out a few more things. Right next to the altar is a small table with the shewbread and the seven-branched candelabrum. Do you see them?"

"What is shewbread? This is all new to me."

"It's specially blessed, unleaven bread, which our scriptures say must always be in the presence of God. It's baked by a Levite family with a secret recipe. The privilege of baking the bread is inherited, passed down to family members of the next generation."

"Interesting. Do the bakers have one of those palatial homes?"

"They certainly live well. Oh look. Do you see the priest sprinkling spices on the fire? The odor of the sacrifice must be pleasing to Yahweh."

"Amazing, and this ritual is supposed to cause Yahweh to forgive their sins. What do you think about all of these practices?"

"I don't think anyone can cause Yahweh. As for me, I ask Yahweh to forgive my sins. I have never sacrificed an animal."

"Good for you, and your point about causing Yahweh is right on target. You know, Lazarus. I must ask you one last question."

"Just one. Are you getting bored with all of this?"

"No. It's fascinating," and Jesus smiled as he looked over at his friend. "But here's what I'm confused about. If you don't believe in animal sacrifice, why are you here?"

"That's an honest question. From time-to-time I sell vegetables in the Court of Gentiles. On market days, the place is full of merchants and potential buyers. I came today to renew my license. It's just another tax."

"Do you live near here?"

"Yes, in Bethany which is a twenty-minute walk from the Mount of Olives. Did you enter the city by going down that steep slope with all the olive trees?"

"Yes, this morning."

"Then you passed quite near my farm. I see now that a priest is sprinkling blood over the sacrifice. We're almost done. Let me point out one more part of the Temple. If you look past the altar, there's a huge door into that structure with the gold columns. That's the Holy of Holies, the place in the Temple where God is believed to live."

"I've heard about that place, and it must be very special; but my God is also present in my native land of Galilee. I can sense my God in the lush meadows that birds inhabit and wildflowers grow in abundant clusters. I also sense this God when I'm with my family and working alongside neighbors I have known all my life."

"You are speaking my language, Jesus, but listen up. Here comes the closing." A priest walked away from the fire to face the spectators. As he stood before the crowd, he gave this blessing.

"The Lord bless you and keep you; the Lord make His face to shine upon you, and be gracious unto you; the Lord lift up His countenance upon you and give you peace."[6] The two friends exited from the Court of Israel along with the other spectators. Once outside in the Court of Gentiles, Lazarus turned toward Jesus and said: "Where are you staying tonight?"

"I haven't made plans yet."

"Stay with us. I would love for you to meet my sisters Mary and Martha. We have a farm in Bethany, no more than a thirty-minute walk from here." Jesus was becoming very fond of this gentle giant with the long gray hair and gray beard. He seemed to be quite vigorous despite his advanced age. He will be good to know, Jesus thought. He can help me understand Temple Judaism, which seemed to him to be quite different from the simple worship at his native village.

• • •

As the sun set in the western sky, Jesus was both hungry and tired. It had been a long day. The tour of Lazarus's farm had been interesting. The fields of olives and grapes encompassed thirty acres with an additional five acres devoted to assorted vegetables. The vegetables were the pride and joy of Martha, a tall, thin, aristocratic woman who looked a lot like her brother. Mary was shorter, somewhat plump, with a round face that was quick to break into a gentle smile. She was the cook in the family.

The smell of lamb broiling in the rock oven as Jesus and Lazarus entered the six-room, one-story house was a welcome smell. Mary was slicing bread at the large table, and as they entered she smiled across at them. "We will begin the evening meal in half an hour. You men will need to wash up."

"Tell me what brought the three of you together?" Jesus asked as they finished with the blessing and were all seated around the table.

"Sadly, each of our spouses has died. I lost my Elizabeth two years ago. Martha's Jonas died about the same time, and Mary lost her Samuel, was it seven years ago?"

"Closer to eight. I'm the ancient one in the family. This farm originally belonged to our father, and when Elizabeth died Lazarus invited us to return home."

"It's been a blessing for all of us," Lazarus said.

"Your story is similar to my own. I lost my Anna last month in childbirth. It was to have been our first child. The loss was so devastating I fled from my home in Nazareth. Now I'm beginning to feel a little guilty about leaving. I'm sure my family is worried about me."

"That's so sad," Martha said. "She must have been very young."

"Not so young, but very beautiful. I'm not sure I'll ever get over her."[7]

"Time helps with that," Lazarus said as he dipped his bread in the gravy surrounding the lamb on his plate. "Why have you come to Jerusalem?"

"It took me a while to figure that out. Without Anna, my job as a mason in Sepphoris has no purpose or meaning. I do have some reading and writing skills. I was thinking I could come to Jerusalem to train as a scribe."

"A noble ambition for one who is so learned," Mary said.

"Well, we'll see. I have some questions about the profession, and I need to return to my family first."

"Did you ever make a mistake copying all that stuff?" Martha asked while smiling over at Jesus. "I certainly would have."

"I concentrated really hard on what I was doing, and I worried about it. I certainly didn't want to change anything God had said."

"But you could have," Lazarus interjected with a sly twinkle in his eye. "I often wonder about the honesty of scribes. They could easily leave out something they didn't like."

"Benjosef, my teacher, was a very religious man. I can't conceive of him changing God's word."

"I'm glad you worked for a good one."

"Not to change the subject, but I would love to know if you ever ran across a prophet named John the Baptist in your travels?" Martha asked.

"Yes, I certainly did. I was baptized by John in the Jordan River two days ago."

"Oh, tell us about him," Mary enthused. "All of our friends are talking about him."

"Well, Mary, I must be honest with you and say I wasn't very impressed."

"Interesting," Lazarus interjected as he passed the jug of wine across the table to Jesus. "Drink up my friend. We want to hear all about John the Baptist. What about him did you find to be so troubling?"

"He seemed angry to me. His basic message is quite simple. Repent because you are a sinner. God's judgment is imminent. Unless you repent, you will burn. I don't think God's intention is to condemn or to lash out at us in judgment. The God I know loves us."

"I agree with you that God loves us," Mary said.

"Do you agree with John that God's kingdom is imminent?" Lazarus asked.

"If I were a betting man, I would say soon, but I don't know when God will intervene and bring us His kingdom. I hope it happens soon, but God works on his own time. The one thing I am sure about is that God's intervention will bring joy not the disaster John's message implies."

"Will God intervene through a messiah?" Lazarus asked.

"I have no idea how God will intervene," Jesus responded, "but I hope it is without violence. We have tried the violent approach several times, and it has never worked."

"If God doesn't send a messiah, what can he do?" Lazarus persisted.

"God is God. He will find the right way. I'm not worried about that. I just can't conceive of a God of love using cruel means to achieve his just goal."

"Well said, Jesus," Martha replied as she smiled over at him. "You would be wasting your time as a scribe. All they do is copy legal documents and sacred scrolls. That sounds rather boring to me. I'd rather be weeding my vegetables. You need to be teaching us about this God of love."

"Can I support myself doing that?"

"You won't need to. You have no family to support. People will take you in just like we are doing tonight," Martha said.

"That's an exciting future to consider."

• • •

Jesus worked alongside Lazarus on his farm for the next four days. The two talked religion and became fast friends. As sunset arrived on the fourth day, Lazarus said to his friend: "There will be no more working. The sabbath is upon us. Tomorrow I will show you Jerusalem. You need to see it at its best when people are resting." The next morning the two men left early for their trip to the holy city.

"Last week you saw the Temple. We'll enter the city from the south side of town as you did last week. It's downhill from here. We can use the gate at the Pool of Siloam. The Synagogue of Freedman is right near there. I imagine they will be having a service."

"Sounds good to me. The Temple is on the north side. Is that right?"

"The northeast corner of town." Arriving at the Pool of Siloam twenty minutes later, Lazarus said. "See that small custom's house alongside the city wall on the right? That place will be busy tomorrow. I pay taxes each time I enter the city with vegetables to sell. That, of course, is in addition to the license I had to purchase the day I met you."

"I guess it was good I was traveling light."

"It saved you money." As the two men entered Jerusalem through the city gate, Lazarus announced some directions. "We'll walk up this short hill on the left. The Synagogue of Freedman is on the right." Five minutes later, they were standing at the back of the synagogue.

"Who is that answering questions up at the front?" Jesus asked.

"It looks like a Pharisee with his fancy robes and sashes."

"I've heard a lot about the Pharisees, and yet I've never seen one in Nazareth. It's like they couldn't be bothered. We're so tiny."[8]

"They're a small group of Jews in Jerusalem who strictly enforce the Laws of Moses. They also establish oral rules to fill out Torah. Many work for the priests at the Temple."

"What does that mean? I don't remember my father talking about oral rules," Jesus reflected.

"Well, today is the sabbath. What does it mean to work on the sabbath? What is work? The Pharisees define work with their oral teachings."

"I see. They seem to perform an important function."

"Let's listen. That man at the meeting is asking about purity laws. He wants to know if violating a purity law is different from committing a sin."

"The purpose of purity laws is to honor God," the Pharisee said in a stern, commanding voice. "You don't want to enter the Temple right after you have slept with your wife. So you immerse yourself in a ritual pool to become clean. Only you will know you are impure. The remedy is simple. On the other hand, sin is different. It is a moral impurity. It is a far more serious matter. To remedy that problem, you must engage in sacrifice to atone for the sin. Only then will God forgive you. To conclude my answer to your question, becoming impure is only a sin if you enter the Temple without immersing yourself. Then you are deliberately violating the will of God."

"Thank you, kind sir. You have eased my mind concerning the many times I find myself in a state of impurity."

"He must have some wife," Jesus whispered over to Lazarus smiling. "Actually I agree with what he said about the purpose of purity rules being to honor God. That's pretty much the same answer I gave to Anna the last time we were swimming in the river."

"That's good to hear, but you may have some difficulty with the many oral rules they invent to define a specific Law. But let's continue our walk." The streets became narrow and dirty as they worked their way uphill. Jesus felt like he had entered a sea of tiny, one-room houses. "This is where most of the craft people live."

"The street sign on the right says Potter's Lane. Does the sign carry any special significance?"

"You guessed correctly. Potters live down there. Now on the left you will see a collection of stalls and tables. Tomorrow this square will be full of merchants hawking their wares. I often rent a few tables. It's a good place to sell wine and Martha's vegetables."

"It must be fascinating."

"Tiresome is what I would call it. Now stick with me for five minutes. I have one more place to show you in the lower city." The two men walked past two blacksmith shops, and then turned right on Cobbler's Lane.

"Do you need to purchase shoes?" Jesus asked his friend with a smile.

"No, but as you can see this is the right place to do that. We're almost at the spot I've been looking for. Let me know when it begins to smell." It didn't take Jesus long to reply.

"I do detect an odor in the air."

"That's the garbage dump. You can see it off to the right. This is the saddest section of the city. It's where the homeless live, and there are lots of them."

"I see what you mean. Look at that poor man going through the garbage. It's so unfair. All that money being squandered at the Temple should be used to help people like him."

"I couldn't agree more. I wonder what the Pharisees would say about his picking through the garbage on the sabbath. Is that work?"

"Are they that mean-spirited?" Jesus asked.

"I really don't know too much about their beliefs. I've just heard a few things."

"Let me go see that man," Jesus said as he checked his right pocket for coins. "I have two denarius here. That man could use them far more than me."

"That's lovely Jesus. I'll wait for you here." When Jesus returned, he looked at Lazarus with anguish.

"There are several more homeless people at the other end. I wish I had brought more money with me."

"I'm not surprised," Lazarus said. "It's a huge problem most people try to ignore."

"God must see these people. I wonder why he doesn't do something to help."

"God's ways are a mystery to me."

"Me too," Jesus responded.

"Well, let's move on. I want to take you to another world." They headed west and further uphill, crossing the aqueduct that ran from the west wall of the Temple through the center of the city. Jesus noticed the roads widened as they headed further west. "When the roads become paved, you will know we are there." Ten minutes later, Jesus exclaimed.

"Wow. Look at those beautiful gardens."

"You can see the city wall on the left. It has a circumference of three and a half miles."

"It's a big city," Jesus said. "These gardens are something special."

"Wait till you see Herod's palace. It's right up ahead."

"Oh, my gosh. It's huge. All in white marble, but the walls are so tall you can't see inside."

"Herod used a lot of tax money to build this thing," Lazarus said. "I wonder who's in it now. His incompetent son, Archelaus, lived here for a while, but Rome replaced him twenty years ago. Now Pontius Pilate is in charge."

"Who's Pontius Pilate?"

"The Roman prefect who rules Judea."

"Maybe he lives here now."

"I guess he does when he's in town, but I've heard he spends most of his time in Caesarea. He probably has an elaborate palace there too."

"This is all about the money we pay to Rome. I say for a second time it should be going to the poor. This is scandalous."

"Wait till you see where all the rich Jews live. They too have marble palaces with elaborate gardens and private pools. Maybe not the size of this monstrosity, but they are plenty big." They were quiet for a few minutes, walking toward the Temple when Lazarus continued: "Here we go. Look at that mansion on the left."

"There are three young girls working in the garden."

"They are most likely slaves. Fathers sometimes sell their young daughters to rich Jews to raise money to pay their debts. Young girls can be slaves until they reach the age of puberty at twelve."[9]

"That's so unfair. Fathers shouldn't have such power over their daughters, but it's pretty much the same in Nazareth." Jesus said as he turned away from the house and headed further up the paved street.

"There are four main families that control the Temple. The High Priest comes from one of these families. This home is owned by one of those families, but not Caiaphas. He lives closer to the Temple."

"I think I've seen enough houses."

"Me too. You know, there's a part of me that feels sorry for these wealthy families."

"Money certainly can't guarantee happiness. It often comes between you and God."

"The problem I see for these priests is that their marriage opportunities are so limited. Jewish law requires priests to marry purebred Jews whose bloodlines go back five generations or more. They must have pure Zadokite lineage, both parents coming from the Zadok family. If they marry outside this family heritage, their sons cannot become priests. The result is that children from priestly families marry their cousin or even a niece. These marriages often don't work out well."

"That does sound limiting. I guess I can't become a priest."

"Your parents did not have Zadokite heritage?"

"Worse than that. My father was a Roman soldier."[10]

"That would certainly be disqualifying."

"Thirty years ago when Judas liberated Sepphoris the Romans counterattacked with vengeance. One of their garrisons made camp in my village which was only three miles from the battle. My mother was betrothed to Joseph, my adopted father. The marriage contract was all drawn up. When the Romans came, like Uriah,[11] my father was sent away to Capernaum where additional Roman troops were stationed. They made him a slave, and for two years, before escaping, he took care of their horses. Pentara, my biological father, was second in command of the Roman troops. He moved in with my mother and stayed with her for a little more than a year. He lost interest when she developed a big belly with me."

"Wow! That's some story. Do you think God cares much about such things?"

"I think people like me will be first in his kingdom. There are a lot of us with a similar lineage in Nazareth and the other Galilean villages surrounding Sepphoris."

"It seems a little silly to think of God caring that much about the lineage of his priests."

"I think he would care more about their being honest and less corrupt. This has been another difficult day for me—first the Temple and now this. I have always looked up to Jerusalem. My employer taught me that God dwells in the Temple. I'm beginning to doubt that. I also learned from Benjosef that Jerusalem was the center of the world. I'm beginning to hope that he was wrong about that."

"As I said to you when we first met, I like Galileans who stir up trouble. You are an honest and a very good man."

Notes

1. 105 feet high.
2. Temple guards came from the tribe of Levi, descendants from Levi, the third son of Jacob and Leah. Levites worked under the priests. In addition to serving as guards, they worked as accountants, custodians, physicians, barbers, bakers, and musicians. Approximately 10,000 Levites worked in the Temple.
3. Caiaphas was the High Priest at the Temple from 25 CE to 36 CE.
4. Hosea 6:6, Micah 6: 6-8.
5. Sadducees were a small party of upper-class Jews who did not believe in the resurrection of the dead or the validity of oral laws to fill out the Law of Moses. They had a conciliatory policy toward Rome.
6. Numbers 6: 24-26.
7. Jewish girls usually married young at age thirteen or fourteen. The Anna in the novel is in her mid-twenties.
8. See discussion of the Pharisees in the Explanatory Notes.
9. This law is designed to protect young girls from a master who might take advantage of them sexually.
10. See discussion of Jesus's birth in the Explanatory Notes.
11. Uriah was the husband of Bathsheba who David sent to the front lines of a battle so that he would be killed. Once this happened, David proceeded to marry Bathsheba. See 2 Samuel 11: 2-21.

## 5: HOMECOMING

Jesus left the home of Lazarus, Martha, and Mary early the next morning as the sun was rising. It was a sad parting because they had been very good to him, but he was anxious to go home. He was ready to get back to Nazareth he thought as he descended the narrow, rugged mountain road on his way to Jericho.

His five-week journey had been healing in most respects. He now could face a life without Anna, though things would never be quite the same. He was relieved he could finally recognize himself. His smile and good cheer for the most part had returned. The one nagging question was what would he do for the rest of his life. He had received hints of new directions on this trip, but no definitive plan.

That plan would become clear, he decided, when he was at home within the warm embrace of his family. So he was in a hurry. "I'll be back, Thaddeus and Hannah," he called out as he skirted around Jericho winding his way along the Jordan River. He would spend one night with Rachel at Askar. Her village would put him halfway home.

With the Jordan River on his right and the foothills of Ephraim-- the city named after the second son of Joseph and Asenath, the Egyptian woman whom the Pharaoh gave to Joseph as his wife--on his left, Jesus was confident he was traveling on the right course. He had received confirmation from a caravan leader telling him the best way to Askar was to follow the Jordan River all the way to Mount Ebal. In reflecting on the history of Ephraim, he was glad no one had arranged his marriage.

His original plan was to walk through the night; but with Ephraim three hours behind him, and with thick clouds hiding the moon making it difficult to travel, he found a cluster of palm trees and stopped for the night. After consuming the remains of Mary's generous provisions, he found a soft spot under the trees and lay down to sleep. He was tired after fifteen hours of travel, so sleep came quickly. It was a sleep, however, made fitful by a puzzling dream.

Images of John the Baptist floated through his awareness. He saw him in the river. He heard him address the crowd. "Even now the ax is laid to the roots of the trees, so that any tree that fails to produce good fruit will be cut down and thrown into the fire."[1] Every time John gave that speech in his dream, a different voice, one that was softer and full of compassion said: "You can do better."

These images of John were followed by images of the High Priest in the Temple. It must be Caiaphas, Jesus concluded, although he had never seen him before. The High Priest in his dream was dressed in a blue ceremonial robe, his waist was girded with a band of blue, purple, and scarlet threads, he was wearing a blue turban on his head, and across his chest was a breastplate adorned with twelve precious stones representing each of the twelve tribes of Israel. These images came from comments Lazarus had made about the High Priest on their way home from Jerusalem the day before. The High Priest in his dream was presiding over an atonement service involving the sacrifice of animals. Jesus watched the penitents bargain for prices, and then he watched the spectators in the Court of Israel, with eyes glazed over, look on as the animal was sacrificed. Following this drama which was repeated three times during the night, the voice of compassion and love would comment: "You can do better."

Jesus awoke early and wet from a light rain. Well, at least, I got some sleep he thought. I made it through that rain. He quickly shed his tunic, and fell into the river. The cool, clear water revived his spirits and renewed his energy. He was on his way just as the sun began to shine streaks of light along the river.

Look at that sparkle, he mumbled as he bit into a large olive he had saved from last night. God is good, but what am I supposed to do? What am I supposed to do better? It was a puzzle, one that he was reluctant to dwell on for too long because he could only imagine it involved an awesome responsibility. He focused his thoughts instead on his family. He hoped they were well and thriving, and wondered if they still worried about him.[2]

Maybe I should have stayed to bury Anna, but it was almost like I had no choice. I just fled. There was no rhyme or reason to it. This journey was helpful, though. It gave me new friends. It gave me time and space to say goodbye to my Anna. It gave me hints about new directions. "Oh God, what do you want me to do? Was it you who was saying I could do better?"

The answer to that question haunted him, but the answer would not come. He was encouraged, however, because he was losing the sun behind a large mountain to his left. He was confident it was Mount Ebal from another set of directions given him by a man on a donkey who passed him a little after noon. He climbed to the summit of Mount Ebal; and then walked briskly down the other side, arriving at Askar at dusk. He asked directions to the community well from a man who had difficulty masking his disdain, which reminded him that he had arrived in Samaria. Fortunately, the directions were right on target, and it wasn't long before he was approaching Rachel's house.

Strangely, there was no one in the courtyard, and the door was shut tight. As he approached the door to knock, he stopped short when he heard a man's voice inside. He rapidly turned around, and retreated into the woods. His first instinct was to continue his journey, but he was tired of travel and hungry. More importantly, he had been looking forward to seeing Rachel. So he sat down behind a large oak tree and waited.

Thirty minutes later the man left. It took another ten minutes for Rachel to come outside. "Oh look," Jesus said to himself. "She has her water jug. She must be going to the well. I'll surprise her there."

"Jesus," she said as he emerged from the clearing with a big smile on his face. "You came back. My good friend has come back."

"Hi Rachel. It's good to see you. This seems to be our meeting place."

"Your timing couldn't be better. I have lamb tonight for my oven. Let's hurry back and put it in."

"You must have been working." Jesus said, and regretted saying it immediately. Rachel looked at him in horror, and then picked up her jug. "Here, give that jug to me. I would be happy to carry it to the house."

"You saw me working?" she asked in a tone filled with anguish.

"Oh Rachel, give me that jug," and Jesus took it from her and started walking toward the house. "I did not come to condemn or judge you."

"I'm so sorry Jesus if I let you down. It's my only way."

"Then God surely forgives you, and I have put it right out of my mind." They were quiet for a time with Jesus leading the way and feeling a little funny that their positions were not reversed. As they entered the courtyard, she took the jug from him and said in a matter-of-fact tone that was disturbing,

"I will be an hour preparing our meal. I would appreciate it if you would spend that time gathering some wood. When the darkness makes that impossible, come to the house and light the oil lamps. We will take our dinner outside in the courtyard." Chastened, Jesus headed back into the woods to carry out her instructions feeling a little saddened that their reunion had started under this cloud of suspicion. Fifteen minutes later the cloud lifted when Rachel found Jesus in the woods and ran to him, placing her arms around him.

"I was embarrassed, Jesus. I'm so sorry for this dreadful beginning."

"There is no need for you to apologize, Rachel," he said as he took a step back from her. "I was the cause of the problem. I'm just happy to have found you again."

"God blesses me because you are here. Come back and entertain me with stories about your travels while I finish cooking our meal."

"I'll join you as soon as I gather one more load of wood." After completing that task, Jesus found Rachel adding onions and carrots around the partially cooked lamb.

"When I thought about this lamb after my customer left, I was worried about leftovers. You have solved my problem. Now tell me about Jerusalem. Was it all you dreamed about?"

"No, Rachel. It was a huge disappointment. It's a sewer filled with a small group of people who are very, very rich, and lots of other people who are without homes and can only eat by picking through the garbage at the dump. God must hate this city so many Jews believe is the center of the universe."

"I think a lot of men in my village would agree with you."

"The Temple was even worse. Oh Rachel, I must tell you about my dream." After meticulously recalling his dream for her, she moved toward the large wooden table and poured two glasses of wine.

"We must celebrate the coming to Israel of God's new prophet. It has been a long time since God has sent a prophet to Israel."

"God is not sending me anywhere."

"He called you in that dream, Jesus. I knew I was in the presence of someone special when you criticized Moses for his teachings on divorce. Your lovely green eyes radiate compassion, and you speak with authority. That's exactly what you must do. Help Jews and us Samaritans understand there really is a better way, that God is all about love and not judgment."

"But I don't want to be a messiah. I don't want to lead people. That always ends in disaster."

"You aren't listening Jesus. God didn't ask you to do that. He asked you to teach his people. God wants you to help us understand how he works, how he loves. He wants you to speak for him. He wants you to be his prophet."

"I don't feel like a prophet. Furthermore, I certainly am not qualified to be a prophet."

"If I recall correctly, that's exactly the way Jeremiah felt, and I'm not supposed to know such things. We don't accept your prophets. But let me tell you this. You speak for God when you tell us how to love. You must explain how a God of love can allow Anna to die and me to live as a whore."

"Don't speak that way, Rachel."

"Well, it's true. We do not honor God by masking the truth."

"I've been struggling with that mystery ever since I fled from Nazareth. I know in my heart God is love. I feel it. I sense it. It is an ever-present reality in my life. The only thing that makes some sense is to say that maybe we have overestimated God's direct control of our world. Maybe, because God loves us, he has surrendered some of his control over our daily lives and has allowed us to live on our own. But in the end it's all mystery. I don't know if I have real answers to such important questions."

"I think you do, Jesus. What you just said was really good. It makes sense, but people need to hear it. There is so much tragedy in the world, which us common folk think comes from an angry God. I want to believe in your God of love. Help people like me understand such a God really exists."

"I know I can do that. That comes easy, but how will I support myself?"

"You won't need much support if you find places to stay with friends like me."

"That's exactly what Martha said the other night."

"Who's Martha?"

"A friend for me to stay with," and Jesus laughed across at her. "She has a sister Mary and a brother named Lazarus. I spent a week with the three of them outside of Jerusalem."

"See how easy it is."

"Martha wants me to do something like what you are suggesting."

"That's interesting, but not very important. What is important is that God wants you to speak for him. He wants you to tell people about love."

"I guess I can do that."

"Not good enough my dear friend. I need a much more positive statement."

"I look forward to going to work."

"Oh, I love you Jesus," and she ran from her chair and threw her arms around him. "Your Anna would be so proud. I know of no better way to honor her. Now you sit right here while I put our dinner on the table." Jesus remained at Rachel's table for three additional days soaking up her encouragement, and laying plans for his very different future. In return for her kind hospitality, he built a fence around her garden to keep animals away and filled her courtyard with wood.

• • •

During the four days they were together, Jesus asked Rachel several times to return to Nazareth with him. "You can start over. No more customers. I will give you my house, and build another." She was tempted, but remained in Askar.

"I would not fit there either. You keep forgetting I am a Samaritan."

"It would do the people in my village good to live with a Samaritan."

"I will come find you if my situation worsens," she said in the early morning of Jesus's departure.

"Promise," Jesus said as he threw his arms around her in a long embrace.

"Yes, I promise. Now go home and start saving your people."

"You have helped me find my way, Rachel. I will never forget you."

"I hope not, now go." Jesus hugged her one last time, and was on his way. He headed due north toward Nazareth. It was the sabbath day, and he smiled. I am honoring you Yahweh by returning to my family. And then, not five minutes from leaving Rachel, he fell to the ground in tears. My family without Anna. It had been four or five weeks since the last time he had cried over her.

With considerable relief that Rachel had not seen this breakdown, he eventually resumed his travels. Slowly his mood shifted as he thought about the road ahead. I'm going to tell my people about the Law. Yes, you find God there, but you also find God in your heart. Loving your neighbor is what the Law is all about.

The same thing is true with our purity rules. The point is to honor God. But that is not the only way to honor God. The practice of compassion, justice, and forgiveness also honors God. These later actions are a more important way to do it.

What am I going to tell them about the Temple? Does God dwell there? Is God really present in the Holy of Holies? I certainly couldn't find him there last week.

One thing I must talk to them about is Rome. We all hate the taxes we pay, and the affect of Roman rule on our culture and values. But we cannot get rid of the Romans. So many false messiahs have tried. Only God can do that. I have no clue how he will accomplish that feat, but it will be soon. While we wait, the best way to beat them is to live in loving communities. Then you hardly notice they are there.

These thoughts cascaded through him, one following the other, as he walked rapidly along the narrow footpaths through the plains of Samaria. I can do this, he concluded. I want to do this, he further concluded. These ideas flow so easily. Rachel says they come from God. Maybe so, but they are also a reflection of who I am.

His goal was to reach the outskirts of Galilee that first day after leaving Askar. It would put him in position to arrive in Nazareth by the late afternoon. The time passed quickly with his mind focused on these lofty thoughts. When his legs gave out late into the night, he found a soft bed of ferns beneath the stars and slept like a baby. It's good to be going home. His mind was at peace.

He awoke as usual at daybreak, and continued along his way with renewed energy and much excitement. When he reconnected with the Jordan River a little later that morning, he removed his tunic for a long overdue bath. The water is considerably warmer than it had been at the waterfall, he thought as a dark cloud of sadness floated through his awareness. Memories of Anna will soon become a common occurrence, he concluded. I must learn to turn them into happy ones, and with that thought he exited the river and was soon again on the mud-paved roads that would take him home.

He passed by the gate at Nain at noon, and remembered the beginning of his journey six weeks ago. Maybe my Anna died for a reason, he thought as he quickened his pace toward home. I couldn't serve God in this new way and be married to her. My life would have been too rich and busy to entertain such lofty thoughts. You know, maybe not. Anna wanted me to use my ability to read in a constructive way. She would have supported me in this endeavor. God works in mysterious ways. The one thing I will never be able to explain to my people is what is behind all that mystery. Moses learned that lesson at the burning bush when he asked God to explain himself. "I am who I am," God had said.[3]

"I am almost at the fields of Joses and Aaron," he shouted out with joy. An hour and a half later he waved excitedly at his brother, and Joses stopped in his tracks. "Jesus, is that you? God be praised. You have returned to us at last," and he ran across the field to embrace his brother and welcome him home.

"You look good, Jesus, though your tunic is worn and tattered."

"I feel good, Joses. I'm so happy to be home."

"Mother will be so happy you are back," he said as the two brothers began walking arm-in-arm the last mile of Jesus's journey.

"Is Mom mad? Did she worry?"

"I would say neither. She understood your need to be alone, and she knew you would come home."

"Good. Bless her kind soul."

"You are just like her Jesus unless you have changed on us these last six weeks."

"Thank you, Joses. I will enter our village with much relief. Did you bury Anna?"

"Yes. The day after you left. I will take you to her grave when you are ready."

"I would really appreciate that."

"We buried your little daughter right beside her."

"Oh, Joses," and Jesus stopped and bowed his head. His eyes flooded with tears. "I never thought about our child. A little girl. She would have been so beautiful. This is going to be so hard."

"Like I just said, we won't go anywhere until you are ready, and you need not worry about explaining your journey. We were surprised about your leaving, but upon reflection it did make some sense."

"That's so nice, Joses," and Jesus moved toward his brother to hug him. "Actually I am ready, and I want to begin at synagogue tomorrow night. I will speak to James about it."

"We will be meeting at the village gate as usual after the evening meal. I know the village will welcome you back and listen intently to what you have to say."

"Joses, my brother, it's so good to be home." Joses slapped his brother fondly on the back before returning to round up his sheep.

• • •

Word traveled quickly that Jesus wanted to speak at synagogue the following night. The crowd that gathered that evening was anxious to hear about his travels and to welcome him back. Philip opened the meeting with a prayer thanking Yahweh for Jesus's return, and then he gave an oral recitation of the return of the Jewish exiles from their captivity in Babylon.[4] "God wants us to come home," he concluded. He then nodded to Jesus, who stood up from the ground and slowly made his way to the front of the crowd of his neighbors and friends who awaited his remarks with eager expectation.

"Friends and neighbors; as those Jews must have felt when they returned from Babylon, it's good to be home. If I have caused you anguish or worry because of my travels, I apologize. When my Anna died with our baby, as you know, I panicked and fled. While I was away from you, one very good thing happened. God gave me a new mission and purpose for my life. I want to begin this new mission by telling you a story I learned from Benjosef, my beloved employer in Sepphoris.

"There once was a man with two sons. One day the younger son, filled with youthful energy and looking for a change, asked his father if he could have his inheritance now. The loving father promptly divided the estate between the two brothers, allowing the younger brother to leave for a distant country with his inheritance in hand.

"This younger brother quickly spent his inheritance on a life of debauchery. With his money gone, in desperation, he hired himself out to a local farmer to feed his pigs. When this venture proved to be unfruitful and he was dying from hunger, he concluded his father's servants were better off than he was. He decided then to return home, to beg forgiveness from his father, and to seek employment as one of his father's servants.

"As the younger son approached his father's estate, the father saw him and was filled with compassion. He ran to his son, threw his arms around him, and welcomed him home. The younger son, though obviously delighted with this warm welcome, was also confused. He proceeded to repeat before his father a speech he had been rehearsing on the way home.

"'Father, I have sinned against heaven and against you. I no longer deserve to be called your son.'[5] But the father would hear nothing of this confession. He ordered his servants to dress his son with the best robe and to provide him with new sandals. He then declared they would celebrate his son's return with a great feast. He praised Yahweh for this wonderful turn of events. My son was lost and now he is found, and with that the celebration began.

"My friends and neighbors of Nazareth, I am that lost younger son. When I entered our courtyard yesterday afternoon, my mother Mary leapt from the loom where she was working to throw her arms around me and to welcome me home. The love shown by my mother and the father in Benjosef's story is God's love. I sinned as did that younger son, but our sins were washed into insignificance by the inexhaustible love of Yahweh. My God and the God of my Anna is this God of love."

As Jesus began to return to his seat on the ground, a man in the audience called out a question. "Jesus, what happened to the older son in your story?"

"Alphie, my childhood friend. I have missed our daily travels to Sepphoris."

"I too, good teacher, and my oldest friend. I am thrilled to have you back. Will we be meeting at our usual place before the cock crows in the morning?"

"I will speak to you about that at the end of this meeting; but let me answer your question, and then I will sit down. To answer your question, the older brother was angry, and refused to attend the celebration. He believed he had done all the right things; and yet despite his loyalty, the father decided to reward the sinner. The father thanked him for that loyalty and for his righteous living, but insisted the celebration go forward. We had lost your brother, but now he has returned, the father said. My heart is overflowing as a result of this glorious day.

"Righteous living is important, my dear friend Alphie, but the love of God is more important still. That love is deep, it is inexhaustible as I said before, and a great mystery."

"What will you be doing with this new mission?" Aaron, the blacksmith asked.

"I will be speaking about God's great love to anyone who will listen."

Notes

1. Matthew 3:10.
2. See discussion of Jesus's family in the Explanatory Notes.
3. Exodus 3:14.
4. Following a decree from the Persian king Cyrus, 50,000 Jews returned to Palestine in 538 BCE from their exile in Babylon.
5. Luke 15:21. This story was taken from Luke 15: 11-32.

## 6: Meeting friends in Capernaum

Two weeks later Jesus left on his first trip to Capernaum. Capernaum was a fishing village on the north shore of the Sea of Galilee. Because it was a two-day journey, he was stopping first at Cana to attend the wedding of his cousin Lydia to Isaac, a carpenter. Breaking up the trip in this way made sense because Cana was ten miles due north of Nazareth and was on the way to Capernaum.

He left Nazareth on a morning that was already warm and promising to be a lot warmer. He was in soaring spirits because of a talk he had with his brother James just before leaving. "Jesus, we all got together as a family yesterday when you and Alphie were in Sepphoris. We no longer want you to work there. It would be a waste of your precious time. We believe in and support your new mission. You have indeed gone through a remarkable transformation in the last few months. You taught us all at the synagogue with authority. Aaron will now take your place in Sepphoris. As you well know, we need someone there to provide us with cash money. Joses can tend to the flocks by himself. You will not be burdening us."

"Oh, brother, that is more than I expected or could ever have asked for. I would be happy to help Joses when I am at home."

"You could prepare your lessons while following sheep," James replied with a smile. "That will be up to you. Our goal is to keep you teaching. Your mother thinks of you as a prophet."

"Mothers always think the best of their sons."

"True; but in this case, I'm beginning to think she may be right." In reliving that conversation which ended no more than half an hour ago, Jesus was aglow with love for his family. It was so much easier to go about this new task knowing his family was behind him.

Though it is fair to say he had never had second thoughts after that dinner with Rachel, he did wonder if he was up to the task. He wasn't formerly trained as a scribe. There were many parts of the Law he was unfamiliar with and could care less about. What troubled him were questions. Would he be able to answer all the questions? His approach would be to shine love on each topic. Maybe that approach would answer the difficult ones he concluded. In any event, that was what God had asked him to do. "I just hope I don't disappoint you, my Yahweh," he said as he looked up at the heavens and smiled.

• • •

An hour into his walk uphill and down, along stone-covered mountain paths, he thought he heard a noise on a rock face to his left. It occurred again. Someone was moaning up ahead of him. He ran forward another fifty yards, and then called out in a loud, clear voice. "I am Jesus of Nazareth. Can I do something to help?" There was no response, and so he repeated his offer.

"Go away. Leave me alone," a man shouted out as he emerged from a cave above from where Jesus was standing. "I am unclean. My village has sent me here."

"Your village is where?"

"In Cana, an hour walk to the north. Leave me alone," he shouted out again. "I am unclean. I am a leper."

"I gathered that from the fact of your isolation. Have you seen a physician?"

"Are you kidding. Who can afford a physician?"

"Although I am not a physician, I would like for you to come down, and let me examine your problems."

"I have no money. When I worked, I worked as a mason."

"I was a mason too. Come down and join me. The least I can do is share some fruit from my haversack. There will certainly be no charge."[1]

"How can you cure me if you are a mason?"

"Just come down, and we can talk about it. I'm going nowhere until I have looked at your skin." Slowly the short, emaciated young man came down from the cliff and joined Jesus on the path. "Follow me back a ways," Jesus continued. "There's a flat rock back there where we can sit together." The man followed behind Jesus.

When they arrived at the small clearing and the rock, Jesus turned to face the man. "Again, my name is Jesus. With whom do I have the pleasure of sharing this rock?"

"My name is Tobias. I guess one would add the leper from Cana." Jesus reached out to shake the man's hand.

"You are not afraid to touch me?"

"No Tobias, because I do not think of you as unclean. Was this problem caused by a sin you have committed?"

"I guess so Master, but I really can't put the events together. The best I can recall is that I stole cattle from a man because my family was starving. Three months later I was expelled from my village. As you can see, it took a while for the leprosy to develop. Maybe God was at first undecided as to whether I had sinned." Jesus was stunned to have been called Master. It took him completely by surprise. He had certainly never thought about himself in that way. Recovering quickly, however, he asked Tobias, "Did you ask for God's forgiveness?"

"Yes, and I also paid my neighbor for the cattle."

"Where is the leprosy? On your face?"

"Yes." Jesus placed both hands on the man's face, massaging it gently. He then examined it closely. Eventually he placed both of his hands on the man's shoulders, smiled at him, and said, "Return to your village Tobias, and clear yourself with a priest. Your leprosy has healed."

"Our village doesn't have a priest."

"Then tell your villagers you were cleared by a traveling teacher from Nazareth."

"And who will I tell the villagers healed me?"

"God has forgiven your sins. He has healed you. Your face is clean. Your only problem is that you can't see it." The man fled up the path ahead of him. "He didn't want my fruit," Jesus mumbled with a smile as he too resumed his travels to Cana, this time following Tobias.

• • •

An hour later the stone covered path widened as Jesus entered the tiny village of Cana. He proceeded directly to the home of Lydia's parents. Almost instantly his attention was diverted by the voice of a young girl calling out to her mother. "Momma, that must be the man who healed our neighbor Tobias." Jesus smiled at the girl and continued on his way. He couldn't help noting, however, that he received some strange stares from women who were working alongside their houses. He arrived at the home of Lydia's parents forthwith. As he expected, everyone was busy preparing for the occasion. He was glad to lend a helping hand.

The wedding feast took place in the evening with the festivities beginning when Lydia was led to the home of Isaac's parents in a torchlight procession. Prior to the parade both bride and groom were anointed with aromatic oils. They were dressed in their finest clothes. The bride wore an ankle length white tunic, with a white shawl covering her head and shoulders, and a crown of flowers around her head. The groom was dressed similarly with the exception of the shawl. The food was abundantly distributed in each of several tables, the wine was plentiful, and the guests were exuberant. Several enthusiastic toasts were made from among them.

As the celebration was drawing to a close, an event took place that took Jesus by surprise, causing him to blush rather deeply. Tobias joined the feast, bathed, with a clean tunic, and a trim beard. He ran to Jesus to embrace him. "Master, you have saved me," he said in a voice that was not meant to be private but was geared to be heard by the wedding guests. "You have given me back my life." The wedding guests cheered loudly.

"Speech," one guest called out. "You need to tell us about this." All eyes were focused on Jesus.

"I don't know what to say," Jesus began. "I ran into Tobias this morning, and encouraged him to come home."

"You healed me so that I could come home," Tobias corrected.

"God healed you, not me. It was an expression of his great love. We have another expression of that love at the wedding of Lydia and Isaac. May their love abide forever for that is what God intends a marriage to be, not a contract between two people, but a permanent expression of the love and goodness that comes from God." The crowd cheered as a somewhat disconcerted Jesus was led by Tobias to meet his wife and four children.

• • •

After spending the night with his aunt Naomi, Jesus left for Capernaum as the cock crowed the next morning. From the directions he had received from Tobias after the feast, he headed east to Magdala, a small city on the Sea of Galilee fifteen miles from Cana. From Magdala, he would enter the Damascus Road which circles the lake. Capernaum was six miles north of Magdala. He wondered if he could make it in one day, and where he would stay.

The walk went quickly because he was enchanted by the Galilean countryside. He climbed gentle hills, quickened his pace through grassy plains, and stopped frequently to refresh himself alongside clear, rushing streams. His favorite season was now, the hot, dry Galilean summer, where almost every night it was possible to sleep outside on the roof of one's house. But the rainy season would come with winter, he concluded. It wouldn't be possible to have this lush green scenery without a lot of rain.

As the sun approached the ninth hour,[2] he wondered about Magdala. He must be near. He knew it was a fishing village on the Sea of Galilee, the fifteen-mile lake that so generously nourished the surrounding area; but he had never been there before. To Capernaum either. That was one reason for taking this trip. He was excited about seeing fishing villages on the Sea of Galilee. As his thoughts were meandering along these lines, he came across a wide river and decided to follow it, hoping it would eventually run into the lake.

Fifteen minutes later he stopped short as he returned to the riverbank after circling a large rock. There was a woman directly in front of him washing laundry in the river. She looked about his age, was tall and thin with long black hair. Attractive, he thought, though he wondered what she was doing out here by herself.

"Sister," he called out. "Will this river take me to Magdala?"

"Just follow it for ten more minutes."

"Thank you. By the way, I am Jesus of Nazareth."

"Nice to meet you Jesus. I am Mary from Magdala."

"Can I ask you why you are out here alone?"

"Because I am demon-possessed. I make my neighbors uncomfortable, so I prefer to be alone. I am possessed by two demons, one given me by a rejected husband, and the other by a father who took advantage of me as a child." She burst into tears and turned away from Jesus.

"Mary, that is so sad," Jesus said in a voice filled with compassion. "Put your laundry aside and come to me with your burdens." She looked up at him, hesitated, and finally, after sensing the deep compassion emanating from his luminous green eyes, moved toward him. He followed suit, moving toward her, and soon Jesus was wrapping his arms around her in a warm embrace.

"Let me hold you one minute for each of those demons that torment you," he said while tightening his embrace. "Demons be gone," Jesus commanded. "Demons be gone." Mary was sobbing. She slowly collapsed onto the ground as Jesus released his grip of her. He sat down alongside her, and gently took hold of her hand. "It took great courage for you to tell me that sad story, especially because of my being a stranger."

"What do I have to lose. My life is ruined," she said as she looked over at him with large brown eyes seeking understanding and fighting back tears. "Everyone knows my story."

"I have a divorced friend who has to service men in order to survive. Has your divorce put you in such a position?"

"No. I've been lucky in that respect. My father owned a fish salting factory in the city. When he died, my older brother Joachim inherited the business. It's the largest such factory in Magdala, and it's very profitable. My brother is more than generous in sharing the profits with me. I think he feels guilty he didn't protect me from my father. My problems with him began almost immediately after my mother died."

"It's so sad to think of you deserted and alone. You told me earlier that people in Magdala are nervous being around you. You will never lose those two demons without love in your life."

"My father ruined me for men. He took advantage of me for five years after my mother died. He wouldn't let me marry. I ran away with Thomas when I was seventeen—no marriage contract or anything like that. We just registered the marriage in the offices of the city. Thomas is not a gentle man, and I had difficulty sleeping with him. We never had children, and so he left me four years after we were married."

"What's he doing now?"

"He's an informal partner with my brother. He hauls salted fish to the port of Acre where it is shipped throughout the Mediterranean. He married again, and has five children."

"Are he and your brother good friends?"

"Not really. The partnership began before we were divorced, and my brother continues to honor it. My brother will be among the first citizens in God's kingdom."

"It sounds that way. How long have you been living by yourself?"

"Six years."

"Mary, that has to change. I will help you find a new life. That will push those demons aside."

"I feel so much better sitting here with you holding my hand. Can I share my bed with you tonight?" she asked with a shy grin before turning her head away.

"No, Mary. I will stay with you at your house, but not in your bed. I loved the comfort of a woman once. My Anna recently died in childbirth. I have given what remains of my life to God."

"That is so noble of you, Master. I am experiencing your God sitting here holding your hand. Can you tell me more about him?"

"It would be my honor. Please come and follow me."

• • •

It was an easy decision for Mary of Magdala to follow Jesus because she had no life in her city with the exception of her brother, but even that could be a problem because of a jealous wife. That night she arranged everything in her house for leaving it, and the next morning she gathered together a few items of clothing which she placed in a haversack. She was ready and eager to leave with Jesus in the morning.

"Have you every been to Capernaum, Mary?"

"Yes, several times. It's a small fishing village which provides my brother with a steady supply of fish to salt. We just stay on the Damascus Road. I don't know if you want to spend time at Genneserat. It's on the way."

"No. Let's make it all the way to Capernaum. How much time are we talking about?"

"No more than two hours."

"Good."

"What will you have me do, Master?"

"Well, I've been thinking about that. Doing God's work is rather new to me. I had no plan to gather followers, and now here you are," and he smiled across at her.

"It doesn't trouble you to travel with a single woman?"

"Women make up half of God's wondrous creation, Mary. Without you women, we men wouldn't last long on this earth."

"I wish more men thought like that."

"They will. We just need to show them a better way. We need to show them what love between a man and a woman really means. Not to change the subject, but I've been meaning to ask. Do you know any people in Capernaum?"

"A few."

"That would give us a start."

"You may want to get in touch with the religious leaders."

"Does a small place like Capernaum have such leaders?"

"I know of one. I haven't met him, but I've heard a lot about him. He is the Hazzan who presides over the public meetings. People often meet at his house. His name is Peter. He's a fisherman."

"Do you know where he lives?"

"Unfortunately, not. We can probably find him around the fishing boats on the shore, however."

"We will start there," and he smiled at his walking companion. She seemed so much better than when he had found her. Maybe the demons were leaving her. Giving her the opportunity for a new life may have been all that was required to start the process of her healing.

• • •

They entered the mud-packed main street of Capernaum a little after the third hour.[3] "It's not hard to tell we have come to a fishing village,"

Jesus said. "All you see around courtyards are nets, hooks, and oars."

"You get to the Sea of Galilee by taking any one of these side streets," Mary said.

"I couldn't do this without you," Jesus said as he smiled over at her.

"We should turn right here," Mary said. "The lake is no more than a quarter of a mile down this hill."

"Lead on," Jesus said. Five minutes later they arrived at the rocky shoreline of the Sea of Galilee. There were five or six boats pulled up on the shore. "Let's go find Peter."

"It's my understanding we can't miss him. He's a huge man with red hair and a red beard."

After passing three boats, Jesus smiled and stepped toward the bow of the twenty-seven foot fishing boat. "Peter."

The massively built man with the long flowing red hair and light blue eyes looked up and responded, "Yes. What can I do for you?"

"My name is Jesus, and I am a teacher of God's love."

"We need more of those," he said with a broad grin.

"I understand you are the Hazzan of Capernaum."

"A Hazzan who can't read. I start meetings by telling stories about our wonderful prophets."

"I'm sure the people of your village appreciate that. Would it be possible for me to speak a few words tonight?"

"Hey mates," he shouted toward the back of the boat. "We got ourselves a guest speaker." Then turning to Jesus, he said. "We start our meetings after the evening meal. I can always use help with the message."

"Thank you very much. I see this as a great opportunity. Now, do you need help with the fishing? It looks like I'm free for the rest of the day."

"Sure. We can always use an extra hand. We pay ten percent of the catch."

"There's no need for that. I would just like to get to know you and your friends a little better before the meeting."

"We shove off in half an hour. Be back by then." Jesus smiled up at Peter, and stepped back from the boat to rejoin Mary.

"There are people I can see. Don't worry about me. I look forward to telling them some of the things I've learned over the last two days."

Jesus hugged Mary, and said. "I'll see you for the evening meal."

"Good luck with the fishing," she said as she turned from Jesus to leave.

Jesus patted her shoulder, turned himself, and called up to Peter, "I'm all set, Captain."

"Then climb aboard. The short one by the stern untangling the net is John, son of Zebedee. His brother James just left to pick up another oar. He must have known we were picking up crew." Peter then looked toward the mid-section of the boat and said. "Andrew, my childhood friend, say hello to Jesus." Andrew was in his late thirties, thin, of medium height, with a sun-worn face and a short, stubby beard. He was folding the small sail to stow in the bow of the boat.

"Welcome aboard, Jesus. I could use another hand folding this sail. Unless the wind comes up, it will be of little use today." Twenty minutes later the five fishermen pulled away from the shoreline. Jesus sat behind Andrew on the starboard side helping to row the boat. The physical exertion felt good. Half an hour later James and John ceased rowing and moved to the stern to throw out the nets. Andrew moved across from Jesus to the leeward side to continue rowing. Peter remained at the helm.

"Jesus, who was that woman you were with this morning," Andrew asked after the boat was again underway and things had quieted down. "An attractive one, she is."

"That's Mary. I met her yesterday in Magdala."

"She's not your wife?"

"No. Just a friend. I invited her to follow along with me."

"And she's not married?"

"She was in the past, but not anymore."

"Strange that a single woman would be following you. Where are you going?"

"No place special. I came to Capernaum because I have always wanted to see it along with the Sea of Galilee. My father lived here for two years as a Roman slave."

"He must have hated the place."

"No. He always said the lake was beautiful—a great place to swim."

"Well there's not much to see. What were you expecting to find here?"

"Just people interested in talking about God."

"That's what you do? Are you some special kind of teacher?"

"For lack of a better word, that will do, though I'm not sure about the special."

"What is it you teach? What do you talk about?"

"I talk about a God of love."

"Does this God judge us?"

"I don't think of him as doing that. When you experience God's deep love in your heart, you judge yourself. You know immediately when something you have done doesn't measure up."

"I like that idea. What about God's kingdom? Is it imminent as so many people are suggesting?"

"I think of it as being imminent, but no one knows for sure. God does not think about time the way we do."

"What will his kingdom be like?"

"All I can tell you is that God will rule. That means it will be a place where love rules, where people share, forgive one another, where they help each other out. It is a place where mercy and justice for the poor will reign. It will be a place of joy. When love rules our hearts, we help to create such a place. Villages like Capernaum can become a part of God's kingdom when love rules."

"I want to make Capernaum part of God's kingdom," Peter bellowed from his position at the helm. "I agree with Andrew. I like what I am hearing from you. Now let's talk about tonight. Can you read?"

"Yes. I was trained by a scribe in Sepphoris."

"Then you read the scripture tonight. Our sacred scrolls have not been read in years. I'm sure they are collecting dust. The people will really appreciate hearing the word of God."

"What scrolls do you have?"

"Isaiah and the Psalms."

"I'll read from Isaiah. It's my favorite."

• • •

Because Jesus refused to accept payment for his work on the fishing boat, Peter insisted he and Mary come for dinner. The two graciously accepted. Following dinner, most of the men and women of Peter's extended family walked the short distance to the village gate that provided access to the Damascus road. Fifty or more residents of Capernaum joined them. Mary had spent the day telling women of the village that Jesus had transformed her life. She had quickly found a way to help him.

Peter opened the meeting with prayer, and then he introduced Jesus. "Friends and neighbors, we are honored tonight to have our sacred scrolls finally read. Jesus of Nazareth has graciously consented to do that. While he was with me on my fishing boat today, he asked if he could speak here tonight. From what we heard on the water, I think you will be interested in what he has to say. He will read tonight from the second chapter of Isaiah."

Jesus moved to the front of the crowd, shook Peter's hand, and smiled at the curious group of people seated on the ground before him. Peter handed him the Isaiah scroll. "As Peter indicated, this reading comes from the second chapter of Isaiah. Jesus concluded the reading with these words.[4]

Yahweh will wield authority over the nations
and adjudicate between many peoples;
these people will hammer their swords into plowshares,
their spears into sickles.
Nation will not lift sword against nation,
There will be no more training for war.

Jesus then handed the scroll back to Peter, who moved to the back of the crowd. "My friends," Jesus began, "'Blessed are the peacemakers; for they shall be called sons of God.'"[5]

"Thank you all for coming this evening, and I promise to be very brief. I know you have a busy day tomorrow, and would like to get back to your families at a decent hour.

"Our problem is the Romans who tax us heavily making the life of poor people increasingly miserable. Often we lose our land as a result of these criminal taxes.

"So what can we do? Judas, son of Hezekiah, said we should serve no other gods but the God of Israel. In trying to make that happen, he rebelled against Rome in Sepphoris.[6] As a result, when Rome counterattacked, my wife Anna lost all of the members of her family. My mother Mary was forced to live with a Roman general. Judas claimed to be the messiah, which resulted in Rome burning Sepphoris. Very few Jews survived Rome's vicious attack. The rebellion led by Anthronges, the shepherd boy, was equally disastrous.

"My friends, violence is not the answer. It sounds tempting as hatred fills one's heart, but it never works. Cities are burned, and innocent Jews are slaughtered. Like many of you here, I believe that God's kingdom is imminent, that it will come within the present generation. If God created this earth, he can surely deal with Rome.

"In the meantime while we wait for God to intervene, we can build God's kingdom in the small towns and villages of Galilee by loving our neighbors. Andrew and I talked about this on the boat today. Yahweh is the great God of love. We work to build God's kingdom when we live that love in our daily lives. When people love and serve their neighbors in small communities, we can forget about Rome quickly. Roman greed and cruelty will no longer be able to touch what is most important about our lives.

"I will be happy to answer your questions."

"Thank you for being brief, kind teacher," a large man with a long black beard shouted out from the back of the crowd. "Here's what I want to know. How can God establish a kingdom without using violence? Do you think the Romans will surrender without, at least, the threat of violence?"

"I don't know what God will do to establish his kingdom. That's his problem, but what I do know is that he is fully capable of doing it. So, I'm willing to leave it to him. My point is that we can control our own destiny by creating communities of love. When you live in such a community, you will no longer pay much attention to Rome."

"How can I ignore Rome," another man shouted out, "when that scoundrel Matthew collects twenty percent of everything I own?"[7]

"Pay him quickly, hold your nose, and then find a river to swim with your wife." A few chuckles followed that answer, but several men left the meeting shaking their heads. Many, however, stayed with Jesus well into the night. He continued fishing with Peter and his crew for four more days. At the end of the week, he left Capernaum with Mary, spending three days with her in Magdala.

• • •

It was a sightseeing visit and learning experience for Jesus with one exception. In the middle of the first night, Jesus heard Mary moaning from her bed in the adjacent room. After ten minutes of listening to her muffled cries, he could stand it no longer. He left his mat on the floor, and entered her bedroom. He immediately lay down beside her and placed his arms around her.

"Mary, my special, special friend. Lay your burdens on me. What is the cause of this horrible suffering?"

"Hold me Jesus. Just hold me." And then a few minutes later, "tighter Jesus. Just hold me."

"Mary you are precious. So deserving of God's love. Come to me with what it is that troubles you."

"It's the first time Jesus. I was a little girl of thirteen. It hurt so bad. I dream of that night whenever I'm stressed or feeling down on myself."

"Feeling down on yourself. What is that all about?"

"The people of Capernaum all wondered about me. Many had ugly thoughts. What is a single woman doing with a handsome teacher from Nazareth?"

"Mary that is their problem, not yours. They have damaged hearts which we will have to try to heal. Peter's friends didn't feel that way. You brought all those people to my little talk. It was a success because of all your efforts on my behalf."

"I can't follow you Jesus. I'm an embarrassment."

"You're the best asset I have. I can't do this work without you," and he held her tighter. "Can you feel God's love, Mary? It's leaving me and going right to you."

"Hold me Jesus. Just hold me," and her sobs slowly subsided. Half an hour later she kissed him gently on the cheek, turned to her side, and closed her eyes. Jesus held her for another fifteen minutes before returning to his mat in the next room. After a pleasant day of further sightseeing, meeting the people of Magdala, and a quiet night of Mary's gentle breathing, Jesus left on the morning of the third day for the return trip to Nazareth.

Notes

1. This was unusual. Most healers in first century Palestine charged for their services.
2. Midafternoon.
3. Midmorning.
4. Isaiah 2: 4.
5. Matthew 5: 9.
6. The attack occurred in 4 BCE.
7. A tax collector like Matthew was a Jew. He paid a price upfront to the Romans for the privilege of collecting taxes. He then went out among his neighbors extorting money from them. In Matthew's case, working in Capernaum, he went around the area selling fishing licenses.

7: Sharing Meals

It was a beautiful fall morning as Jesus set off from Nazareth on another trip. His first stop was Cana where he would spend the night with Nathanael, a new follower who would join him on the trip to Magdala and eventually to Capernaum.

"Do I have a movement?" he asked himself with a grin as he walked rapidly along the narrow dirt path. Yahweh must be helping me, he reflected. I wouldn't be able to do this alone. It certainly is a ragtag group. Though we have never bothered with establishing a formal organization, we do seem to have two centers for our work. My, oh my, life has changed for me in the last six months.

The first center was Nazareth. James has been such a big help, and Jesus smiled with gratitude as he thought about his brother. James has worked hard to spread the message in Nain, Japha, and several other surrounding villages. More importantly, he sets such a good example. He lives God's love with his passionate commitment to economic justice and helping others.

The second center was Capernaum. Capernaum's location placed it in the middle of several fishing villages on the Sea of Galilee, but most important were his many friends there. Peter, John, James, and Andrew had been with him from the beginning, and now they were joined by Matthew and Judas. Matthew was the most amazing addition, and Jesus smiled deeply when he thought of this burly tax collector who gave up his position because he wanted to learn how to love God. Judas had his own strengths. He was a hard worker with a keen mind. All six of them traveled the lake region singing the praises of Yahweh, the wonderful God of love.

Nathanael in Cana was also an interesting one. He was the Hazzan there, and had performed the wedding ceremony for Lydia and Isaac. He had originally grown up in Tiberias, but his parents moved to Cana when Herod Antipas, the tetrarch of Galilee, moved the capital from Sepphoris to Tiberias in 19 CE. Nathanael's father hated the Romans and feared their increased presence in Tiberias when it became the capital. They chose to relocate in Cana because Nathanael's mother had family there.

There was one important plus to this family history as far as Jesus was concerned. Nathanael's father had wanted him to become a scribe, so at an early age Nathanael was apprenticed to Mattathias, a prominent scribe in Tiberias. Under Mattathias's careful tutelage over several years, Nathanael had become thoroughly trained in Jewish scripture.

Jesus often thought their roles should be reversed with Nathanael the one leading the way. "You have taught me so much, Nathanael," Jesus said to him at their last meeting three weeks ago. "I couldn't do this without you. You should be the one out there in front of the people."

"Oh, no, kind Master. There's no one who could replace you. Those wonderful green eyes speak for you. They are so full of compassion. They penetrate and warm the heart of everyone you gaze on. God gave me a good mind. It's my great honor to use it to assist you. But the people of Galilee need your heart more than my mind. The love that comes from your heart touches every person you encounter."

Jesus thoroughly enjoyed staying in their house. In addition to Nathanael, Sarah, his wife, was a special woman. She was strikingly beautiful, and so proud of her husband's learning. She reminded Jesus of Anna. The one cloud that hung over their marriage was that after ten years Sarah was childless. He respected Nathanael for remaining with her. Nathanael agreed with him on divorce.

As Jesus approached their home a little before noon, Sarah was in the courtyard baking bread. "Jesus," she shouted out with joy, "my dear friend and Master. We have been eagerly awaiting your arrival. Nathanael is in the orchard pruning the grape vines."

"Let me join him there," Jesus responded as he entered the courtyard and embraced his friend. "You look wonderful, my dear Sarah. Can I do anything to help you before I go pick the brains of your scholarly husband?"

"What you can do for me is teach my scholarly husband to read scripture and then laugh. He is so serious about his studies. You always tell us God wants us to laugh."

"I will tell him, Sarah."

"Now before you go, let me make a lunch for the two of you. You can bring it to Nathanael and save me a trip." Jesus happily took the lunch, which the two men devoured with pleasure. After finishing, they spent the rest of the afternoon discussing the prophet Amos.

"I love Amos," Jesus said as the two men were aimlessly wandering home as the sun was setting low in the western sky. "He is so right about Yahweh's love of justice and helping the poor."

"Amos is so right about many things Jesus."

"I know. As I have said many times in the brief period in which we have known each other, you have taught me well. Now, what will we tell Sarah about the afternoon?"

"The truth, of course, that we lost track of time reflecting on the oracles of Amos. She will understand. You are her hero, Jesus."

"She may think more highly of me if I tell her I tickled you and made you laugh during the course of our study."

"That would do wonders. She teases me constantly about my serious approach to scripture. 'Now Nathanael. God can wait. It's time for you to take me out in the flowers.'"

"She's a good woman. Do you think she would like to join us tomorrow?"

"I don't know the answer to that question. We can ask her when we get home."

• • •

The three companions left for Magdala the next morning, arriving there just in time for the evening meal. Mary, hoping that she had the right day for their visit, had gone overboard in preparing a delicious fish stew. Jesus was thankful Sarah had joined them because she was a healthy role model for Mary. The two women instantly bonded with each other. Jesus was hopeful Sarah's upbeat, natural pleasantness would help to lighten what darkness remained with Mary's disposition. Though she was not quite there, Jesus was proud of the progress Mary had made.

The following afternoon he was both proud and grateful to Mary for organizing what turned out to be an event. She had talked about Jesus's coming to the people of Magdala for a week. She had even set a time, the tenth hour,[1] and a place, the Magdala shoreline, for the meeting. As the tenth hour approached, Jesus walked toward the shoreline and was amazed at the size of the crowd.

"You do good work, Mary," Jesus said as he smiled across at her. They were walking together with Nathanael and Sarah.

"I think of it as God's work. God's love, which you have helped me discover, has changed my life."

"It changes everybody," Jesus responded.

"I think we need to put you on a boat Jesus," Nathanael said as the four companions descended the small hill to the lake. "If you stand on the bow, every one will be able to see you."

"That's fine, until something happens to rock the boat."

"It's pretty calm out there. The only thing that may rock the boat is your message. I'm going to walk into the crowd and find a fisherman who will let us do it."

Twenty minutes later as Jesus climbed onto the bow of a brown-hulled fishing boat, the crowd moved toward him and quieted down. "Good people of Magdala, thank you for coming this afternoon, and thank you, Mary, for making it all possible." He quickly spotted Mary up front, and smiled at her.

"This afternoon I want to talk about being poor, something all of us here know something about. It is my belief that we will be first in God's kingdom. 'Blessed are you who are poor, for yours is the kingdom of God.'[2]

"Why? Why will the poor be the first ones to experience God's kingdom? Simply because our economic situation forces us to share. You share fishing nets. There is one baking oven in a courtyard that serves several families. Wine presses are shared as are weaving looms. In my village of Nazareth, one shepherd tends the flocks of several families. The tools of our trade are shared.

"As far as God is concerned, the most important thing is to learn to share with love. Try to push aside petty grievances you may hold toward your neighbor. Work with a neighbor, provide assistance to a neighbor, be concerned with the well-being of a neighbor, refrain from competing or judging a neighbor.

"When one serves a neighbor in this way, God's love becomes a reality. When God's love rules, you will be living in his kingdom. Deep joy comes from living in such a community. Sharing with love is the first step in creating God's kingdom. Because our economic situation forces us to share, we are advantaged when it comes to creating a place where God's love rules."

Though he had planned to direct his comments in a somewhat new direction, his train of thought was interrupted by a question from the crowd. A large man with a long gray beard sitting up toward the front asked: "Good teacher, is it a sin to be rich? I have wanted to become rich all of my life."

"There is nothing inherently evil about wealth," Jesus responded. "The problem comes when getting rich dominates your focus, when you become obsessed with the accumulation of wealth. When that happens, you have no room for God, your neighbor, or anyone else for that matter. People become objects you use in obtaining your objective.

"We find God when we love him and serve our neighbor. We push God out of our lives when we use people and become obsessed with obtaining material things. A society organized around sharing helps us to focus on what has lasting value."

"It would be a whole lot easier to build God's kingdom if we could get rid of the Romans," another man shouted out.

"That question seems to come up in every setting. As I have said before, the best way to put the Romans out of your mind is to create and live in a loving community. It's so easy to ignore them then."

"I just can't stand the wealthy," another man yelled out. "All they want to do is to keep us poor and subject to them. They say we must be sinners because God hasn't blessed us with riches."

"Be careful about hating anyone my good friend," Jesus responded with a warm smile. "Hatred in your heart is poison. It contaminates you rather than touching the object of your hate. You will only be hurting yourself. Hate your conditions, but not those people who live differently." The questions kept coming, one after another, and it was getting late. Finally, Jesus ended them.

"Thank you all for coming. I'm amazed so many of you are still here. Now I don't know about you, but I'm getting hungry. Let me suggest that our women quickly run home and bring back wine and one item to share. We will celebrate the goodness of life and the coming of God's kingdom by sharing a meal together."

• • •

A week later a much smaller common meal was shared at the home of Peter and his wife Sapphua in Capernaum. It was a party to say goodbye to Nathanael and Sarah who were returning to Cana the next morning. All of Jesus's committed followers were there with the exception of James who had remained in Nazareth.

As Sapphua filled his bowl with lamb stew, Jesus raised his wine glass and said: "Next time I come I promise to bring James. We are as different as oil and water. James drinks no wine and refuses to eat meat. He has allowed no razor to touch his beard much to the chagrin of his good wife. He is devoted to the Law, and yet his devotion to the poor is the central focus of his life. He thrives on telling people about Yahweh, the God of love. The God that James proclaims seeks no revenge, or judgment. Sin is a human shortcoming that God forgives. I think you will like him."

"Please make good on your promise, Master," Philip said. "Tell your brother we all look forward to meeting him."

"Well said, Philip," Peter replied. "I would like to raise my glass and welcome you aboard as our newest member. Philip asked to join us after John and I spoke at a meeting in Bethsaida. Philip told us he was tired of being labeled a sinner."

"You came to the right place," Matthew said looking at Philip with a warm smile. "We are all sinners here."

"Excuse me," James, son of Zebedee, interjected with a laugh. "Who says I'm a sinner? I'm a fisherman. My family has fished in the Sea of

Galilee for three generations. It occurs to me every day I work for Jesus that I am fishing. We go out to catch people and tell them about our God of love."

"Yes, but it's catch and release," his brother John chimed in. After the laughter subsided, Judas raised his glass to praise Mary.

"Yahweh could not have caught a better fish when Mary came into our fold. She is the best organizer in our group. Jesus, your ears must burn when Mary is out talking about you." Mary instantly burst into tears. Sarah, who was sitting beside her, held her in a warm embrace. She buried her head against Sarah's shoulder before lifting it and smiling across at Judas.

"I have found a new family and a new life," Mary responded before tears again poured forth from her soft, vulnerable eyes.

"We have all found a new family," Jesus said. "I can't tell you how much you all mean to me. You have filled the void left by Anna's death. I was thinking moments ago when Judas was praising our Mary about the meaning of a common meal like this."

"Don't ruin all this good food with a speech," Peter said with a laugh.

"I won't be long, but let me tell you briefly about my experience at the Temple in Jerusalem. As you know, Jews believe Yahweh resides there in that special room they call the Holy of Holies. The only person to ever enter that room is the High Priest during the Yom Kippur celebration. Why is access to God limited to the High Priest? I did not find God in that lavishly decorated viewing area watching innocent animals being slaughtered for no other reason than to appease an angry God. I find God here. God is present in this courtyard because we love one another and are sharing a meal together. That pompous High Priest has no monopoly on access to our God of love."

"You are back to the book of Amos, good teacher," Nathanael interjected. "I think I can recite him verbatim.[3]

I hate and despise your feasts,
I take no pleasure in your solemn festivals.
When you offer me holocausts,
I reject your oblations,

And refuse to look at your sacrifices of fattened cattle.
Let me have no more of the din of your chanting,
No more of your strumming on harps.
But let justice flow like water,
And integrity like an unfailing stream."

"That's it exactly, Nathanael," Jesus said.

"Let's go to Jerusalem for the Feast of Lights," Philip said. "It's in two months. The winter is a slow time anyway. I've never been to Jerusalem, and would like to see this corruption for myself."

"My brother James needs to see it too," Jesus said. "I think you have a very good idea."

Notes

1. Late afternoon.
2. Luke 6: 20.
3. Amos 5: 21-24.

## 8: The Feast of Lights

The contingent of followers from the Sea of Galilee arrived in Nazareth, minus James of Zebedee who remained in Capernaum to fish, on the sixteenth day of Kislev.[1] They remained in Nazareth for two days. Jesus was thrilled for these special friends to finally meet his family. They brought with them provisions for the trip, travel money they could spare, and tents to keep the cold wind out at night. Alphie and Jesus's childhood friend Aaron each loaned the travelers a donkey to carry the heavy items on the trip.

On the eighteenth day of Kislev, the travelers set out for Jerusalem. The Feast of Lights was celebrated for eight days beginning on the twenty-fifth. Jesus wanted to attend the Temple ceremony on the first day. He also wanted to have supper with Lazarus and his family before the festival began. His goal was to arrive at Bethany on the twenty-second, which meant walking, on average, twenty miles a day. It was a tall order, but this schedule left an extra two days if they were delayed for some reason.

The only two members of the group who had ever been to Jerusalem were Jesus and Nathanael. The others had no idea what they were in for, but they were giddy with excitement. Sarah led them in song.[2]

Shout for joy, all virtuous men,
Praise comes well from upright hearts;
Give thanks to Yahweh on the lyre,
Play to him on the ten-string harp;
Sing a new song in his honor,
Play with all your skill as you acclaim him!

The word of Yahweh is integrity itself,
All he does is done faithfully;
He loves virtue and justice,
Yahweh's love fills the earth.

Nathanael related the history of the festival. "It celebrates the triumph of the Maccabees over the Syrians. King Antiochus 1V Epiphanes of Syria became king in 175. Upon ascending the throne, one of his first acts was to invade Judea where he both looted the Temple and laid waste to Jerusalem. He outlawed Jewish sacrificial services, ordering pigs to be sacrificed instead. He further profaned the Temple by erecting an altar to Zeus. When the Maccabees threw out the Syrians in 165, Judas Maccabeus ordered the eight-day ceremony to celebrate their victory and to rededicate the Temple.

"The date of the twenty-fifth of Kislev was set by Judas to honor Nehemiah. Nehemiah was appointed Governor of Judea by the Persian king Artarerxes in 535 with a mandate to rebuild Jerusalem and the Temple following the Babylonian captivity. Nehemiah relit the altar fire in the Temple on the twenty-fifth day of Kislev. The Feast of Lights, also known as Hanukkah, is celebrated in the Temple with services of sacrifice and the lighting of one candle on the altar Menorah for each of the eight days."

"Your husband knows so much about our history, Sarah," Mary whispered across to her traveling companion. "You must be very proud of him."

"I am," Sarah replied. "Mattathias trained him well. I wish he could become a scribe, but he was never formally trained, and we are poor so he must farm."

"Nathanael," James, the brother of Jesus, called out. "Is Hanukkah a sabbath-like holiday? Or can you work during the eight days of the celebration?"

"You can work. There is, of course, at least one sabbath during that eight-day period."

"What about the service in the Temple?" John asked. "What can we expect to see?"

"The service focuses on the lighting of one candle on each of the eight days, and the atonement ritual where an animal is sacrificed. Remember that Antiochus banned sacrifices. Hanukkah celebrates bringing sacrifice back as a central focus of worship."

"Antiochus was one cruel king," John concluded. "But he may have been right about sacrifice."

"You seem to have taken my view on that John," Jesus said as he shifted his focus from the narrow footpath ahead and turned toward John. "Hold off on your opinion until you see it for yourself. We can talk about the matter further then."

"I would like to discuss it further with you, Master. I'm just glad we don't sacrifice fish."

"Nathanael, I was telling your wife a moment ago how impressed I am with all of your knowledge. You are preparing us well for this visit. The history of our people is a fascinating topic I would like to learn more about."

"Well, thank you, Mary. Comments like that make all of my past studies worthwhile."

"I do have one question for you, Mary said."

"I will try my best to answer it."

"Why are there eight candles?" Nathanael broke out in a belly laugh. Sarah smiled in deep appreciation. Maybe he is learning not to take himself quite so seriously she thought to herself.

"Here you are praising me, and I might be stumped. I think it goes back to the Maccabean revolt. When the Maccabees liberated the Temple, they found that almost all of the olive oil to light the Menorah was gone. They thought they only had enough oil to keep the candle lit for one day, but it lasted for eight. It was something like that anyway."

"That's good enough for me," Mary responded with a smile.

"Nathanael," the deep, sonorous voice of James bellowed out one more time. "Didn't that cruel king kill all Jews who circumcised their male children?"

"Yes he did. It was his goal to destroy our religion. We owe the Maccabee brothers a lot."

With songs to sing and history lessons to learn, time passed quickly on that first day. They camped long after dark beside a river on the Samarian plains. The second day started off well with Sarah again leading the group in song. It wasn't long, however, before a problem arose.

"Jesus, I think it is time we headed east toward the Jordan River," Nathanael said.

"The distance is shorter if we keep heading south toward Mount Ebal. There's a village near the summit called Askar. I thought we could stay there tonight," Jesus responded.

"Is Askar Samaritan?" Peter asked. "Are you suggesting we stay with Samaritans?"

"It takes ten miles off the trip, and I want you to meet my friend Rachel. She saved my life six months ago when my Anna died." On hearing this conversation, James left Andrew with whom he was walking, and caught up with Jesus.

"It's an abomination for Jews to interact with Samaritans, my brother."

"If God is all about love, that love is big enough to include Samaritans. If you want to take the long way, then you can begin heading east for the Jordan River. I will meet you in Jerusalem."

Though Jesus may not have meant to hurt his brother's feelings, James returned to Andrew chastened. He was silent for most of the rest of the day. He returned to walking with Andrew, however. He and the rest of the travelers continued to follow Jesus.

• • •

To put it mildly, Rachel was shocked when Jesus and his band of weary travelers arrived in Askar a little before dusk. Rachel did not disappoint Jesus, however. She fed the exhausted walkers, and listened attentively to stories about their trip. After the evening meal was over, Jesus approached Rachel and said: "Leave the cleaning up for Mary and Sarah. You have done your part. Let's you and I take that water jug and fill it at the well." Jesus continued his conversation with her as the two friends left the courtyard. "You look well Rachel. How is life treating you?"

"Much better, my dear teacher. You have made me feel good about myself again. Some of my old self-confidence has come back. It has allowed me to return to my village. I spend more time there, and you will be happy to know I have a new business."

"Oh Rachel, your news warms my heart."

"I'm taking care of children. The wife of my former husband died from some strange fever. They have four children, and Jacob needs help. We may even get back together. I loved him once as a very young woman, and he is nice to me again. We'll see."

"I'm proud of you Rachel," and he set the water jug down on the ground so he could embrace her. "You are a very special woman."

"It was your love that helped me learn to think differently about myself."

"We saved each other."

"And now look at you, Jesus," Rachel said laughing. "Sarah thinks of you as a prophet, and her friend Mary says you're just like God. You're leading a movement just like I knew you would."

"I hope I am doing God's work."

"Stop that Jesus. You know you are."

When the two friends returned to Rachel's house, several of the weary travelers were sound asleep. Jesus borrowed an extra blanket from Rachel, and joined Andrew, Nathanael, and Sarah on Rachel's roof. Though it was a cold night, the roof offered Jesus the opportunity to look out at the stars. "I hope you are watching over us, God," Jesus spoke quietly after finishing his prayers. "My heart and my Rachel tell me you are blessing my work. It is my honor to speak about your love," and he slowly drifted to sleep. He slept soundly, awakening only when Andrew gently shook him and suggested they should probably think about leaving.

As they said their goodbyes to Rachel half an hour later, Jesus was proud of his younger brother. "Rachel, we so enjoyed that evening meal and your gracious hospitality," James said while smiling deeply. "We would be honored if you would accompany us to Jerusalem."

"Thank you, James. That's a tempting offer, but I have four children to take care of in my village. I need to send you on your way right now." Jesus stepped forward to hug her.

"We will be back, Rachel. I promise."

• • •

The trip to the home of Lazarus, Martha, and Mary was uneventful. When they arrived there just as the sun was setting on the twenty-third of Kislev, Lazarus was thrilled to welcome them into his home. "You make our home your base for the next eight days. We have plenty of room. Some of you can sleep in the barn. There is an extra room there. We can spread out hay."

"That's very nice of you, Lazarus," Peter said as he held out his hand for Lazarus to shake in greeting. "But I must tell you what we fishermen say about guests. Like dead fish, after three days they begin to smell." Lazarus smiled, but he would have none of that.

"After three days at the Temple, you will all be ready to work for me."

The Galileans thrived at the home of Lazarus. Mary and Sarah worked together with Mary and Martha as if they were adopted nieces. They helped with the cooking, and with a hooked rug Martha was making for the extra bedroom in their house. The male Galileans enthusiastically accepted Lazarus's condition, and worked to clear a new field for him when they were not being Jerusalem tourists.

Work on the twenty-fifth of Kislev stopped, however, well before noon. Bodies and tunics were washed; and after a hasty lunch of leftovers from the previous evening, fifteen expectant communicants headed west for the two-mile walk to the Temple.

The trip was all down hill, and the scenery was beautiful. They saw the Dead Sea and the Jordan River off in the distance. On both sides of them, as they walked toward the imposing Temple which never left their sight, were groves of olives. Lazarus turned to Sarah and smiled. "You are traveling down the Mount of Olives. As you look around, you now know why."

Thirty minutes later, Lazarus stopped the group and said: "You have entered the Garden of Gethsemane. It is one of the prettiest places in the city of Jerusalem. It also tells us we are almost there." The group went off in different directions admiring the garden with Lazarus taking Jesus aside to a collection of palm trees. "I almost forgot to tell you, Master. John the Baptist was executed about a month ago. Antipas accused him of being a revolutionary."[3]

"That's sad news, Lazarus."

"I know you differed with him," Lazarus responded.

"Yes, but he was a very good man—devout, righteous, single-minded, and certainly charismatic. The one thing he was not was a revolutionary."

"I wish I had heard him. The three of us talked about making the trip to Jericho, but never got around to it. I guess we're getting old. It's not an easy trip as you so well know."

"You may have missed a dramatic performance."

"I think you're right, but I do not want to miss another one. Hey everybody," Lazarus called out. "Come join me. We need to get to the Temple before the sun sets. We lose the sun early at this time of year."

The group gathered and walked the remaining 500 yards to the east wall. They entered the Temple grounds at the portico of Solomon, paid the half shekel Temple tax, and then the males and females split, the women turning a sharp left and the men veering to the right to separate ritual pools. Their purpose was to purify themselves through immersion in the baths.

Once that was completed, Martha came up to her brother. "Let's all go to the Women's Court so we don't get separated. There may be a thousand people here or even more. I've never seen it this crowded."[4]

"That's what I was thinking too." Lazarus turned away from his sister and faced most of his guests. "Hey there everyone. As you can see, there are lots of people here. Try to stay together because you will have a difficult time finding the farm by yourself at night.

"We are currently in the Court of Gentiles which circles the Temple complex. We will watch the service from the Women's Court which is open to both males and females. Follow the crowd because most of them are going there too. We cross this expanse and enter the Temple proper by climbing the stairs you can see over my shoulder and to the left."

As Lazarus led the Galileans up the marble steps into the Women's Court, his guests were wide eyed with amazement. "I can't believe these marble walls with plates of gold. Magnificent," Phillip said mostly to himself.

"It came from fifty years of Jews paying taxes," Judas responded.

"I hope we can see the ceremony with all these people here," Andrew said.

"We should be fine," Lazarus reassured him.

"The ten Menorahs on the altar are beautiful," Sarah said.

"They will light the first candle on each one at the beginning of the ceremony," Lazarus said. "It shouldn't be long now. Our timing is pretty good."

Ten minutes later a hush fell over the crowded Court as the High Priest, dressed in a long white robe with small gold bells sewn into the fine linen, entered the sanctuary. His waist was girded with a band of blue, purple, and scarlet threads, and across his chest was a breastplate adorned with twelve precious stones, one for each of the tribes of Israel. He wore a fine blue turban on his head. He was followed in a solemn procession by several priests dressed in spotless white tunics and turbans of red.

"Is that fat guy leading the procession the High Priest?" Peter asked Nathanael as the group of dignitaries moved past them.

"Hush now Peter or you will get us thrown out."

"That gaudy costume is disgusting." To Nathanael's relief, the costumed men were soon at their places by the altar, and Peter remained silent for the moment. The High Priest turned to face the audience. "Is that Caiaphas?" Peter asked, this time in a whisper. "That guy needs to go on a diet." Nathanael turned toward Peter and placed a finger to his lips signaling silence.

"Welcome to the first evening of our Festival of Lights," the High Priest intoned in a deep, loud voice that carried easily throughout the large hall that made up the Court of Women. "The priests will now light the first candle." Three priests moved toward the altar to perform that function for each of the ten Menorahs.

"We are happy to rededicate our hearts and our Temple to Yahweh at this time," the High Priest continued following the lighting of the candles. James stood there impressed with the service until the sacrifice of the animal took place. Three priests moved toward the large fire, throwing slabs of meat directly onto it. This was followed by a fourth priest who sprinkled aromatic spices into the flames. It was important that the odor be pleasing to Yahweh. While all this was going on, the Levite choir sang in the background.

"Is that all fat boy has to say?" Peter whispered across to Nathanael. "He's not so bad after all."

"Do you like things to be brief, Peter?" Nathanael responded with a smile.

"Yahweh gets bored with windbags."

Sarah, standing next to her husband, asked quietly to no one in particular "Where did the slaughter take place?"

"Somewhere quite close to this Court," Martha responded.

"What happens to all the blood?" Judas piped in. "They must generate a lot of it over the course of a festival like this."

"There is an elaborate drainage system that runs downhill and out of the Temple complex," Lazarus responded. As the ritual unfolded, Lazarus pointed out the Holy of Holies as well as the Antonia Fortress and the Sanhedrin,[5] two formidable structures connected to the Temple and clearly visible from the Women's Court. It wasn't long before he quietly announced to his guests that the service was coming to an end. "The two priests sprinkling blood on the fire tell us that the service is about over." It wasn't long after he spoke that the High Priest moved forward to give the closing benediction.[6]

"May Yahweh bless you and keep you.
May Yahweh let his face shine on you and be gracious to you.
May Yahweh uncover his face to you and bring you peace."

As Jesus moved with the other spectators to exit the Court, he turned to James and said: "What I want is love, not sacrifice; knowledge of God, not holocausts. Hosea said that."[7]

"Hosea said it well, brother. May you always go in peace."

• • •

With the next day being the Sabbath, the group stayed mainly around the house and visited. It was cold and rainy which made the decision easier. Jesus wanted to honor the wishes of James and Lazarus for whom the rules about work were important.

The following two days were different. The eleven-man crew worked hard clearing the new field for Lazarus. They came near to completion. The women visited and worked with Martha on the rug. As they awoke on the twenty-ninth day of Kislev, Lazarus announced there would be no working today. "I am sending you to Jerusalem. You have exhausted me over the last two days," he related to them with a smile. "I will rest here and await your return."

The group went out in different directions. With Jesus were Nathanael, Sarah, Peter, and John.

"Nathanael," Jesus said. "I'm going to take you to the Synagogue of Freedman. I'm hoping the Pharisees are there. I would like you to meet them and see what you think. Lazarus introduced them to me the last time I was here. I'm glad James decided to go with the other group because he might have joined them."

"Sounds good to me, Master. I've heard a lot about them, but I have never met one."

The group of five arrived at the Tower of Siloam on the southern end of the east wall of the city forty-five minutes after leaving the home of Lazarus. They entered Jerusalem at the gate there, and immediately turned left for the short uphill climb to the synagogue. Jesus was not disappointed. There was a small group of men standing outside the synagogue, again dressed in fancy robes and sashes, answering questions for several people who had gathered around them. The five Galileans joined the discussion.

"Good teachers, would one of you kindly clear up a question that has been puzzling me ever since we moved to a house closer to the Jordan River. Of things that live in water, what creatures are we allowed to eat?" A tall Pharisee standing to the right of the Galileans stepped forward.

"Are you here for the Feast of Lights?"

"Yes we are," the man replied. "My wife and our three children came with me to the festival and to visit family."

"Welcome to God's city, kind sir."

"Well I guess it would be more honest to say welcome back. We moved just outside of Jericho three years ago. But we are certainly enjoying our return to Jerusalem."

"May Yahweh be praised. Now to answer your question. The Lord says that anything with fins and scales living in the sea, a river, or a lake may be eaten. But any creatures without fins or scales, you must not eat for God finds them to be detestable."[8]

"Thank you, kind teacher. As always, Yahweh makes good sense."

Another man who was standing right in front of the Galileans spoke next. "I too have a question from Leviticus. Moses teaches us there that Yahweh wants us to love our neighbor as ourselves.[9] Who is our neighbor?"

"I can answer that question," Jesus said as he moved toward the front of the group. He turned around to face them and said: "Let me tell you a story.[10] The story was inspired by a woman living in the village of Askar, a two day walk to the north from here. This woman is one of the finest people I know.

"As you all know, the road from Jerusalem to Jericho can be a dangerous one to travel. A man left from here one day on his way to Jericho and was quickly overtaken by brigands. These thieves took all he had and beat him badly, leaving him on the side of the road to die.

"The first person to pass the man on this sad day was a priest who ignored the man. Despite hearing his moans, he passed by on the other side. This priest was followed by a Levite who reacted the same way, passing the injured man on the other side.

"Some time later a Samaritan traveler came upon the man and was moved by compassion. He bandaged his wounds, pouring oil and wine on them. He then offered the man his donkey and brought him back to his home in Jerusalem."

Looking directly at the man who had posed the question, Jesus asked: "Which of the three men in this story fulfilled the requirement to serve his neighbor?"

"The answer is obvious, good teacher. The Samaritan who bandaged the man and carried him back to his home in Jerusalem."

"You are an astute observer my good friend. Now you can answer your own question about who is your neighbor from hearing this story."

"The man at the side of the road who was injured."

"Yes, again," Jesus replied. "Our neighbor is anyone we find to be in need of help. Now go out yourself and find such neighbors." Jesus smiled at the man who had posed the question as he returned to his friends at the back of the crowd.

"This man is not a good teacher," the tall Pharisee mumbled to his colleague standing next to him. "He honors Samaritans while vilifying our Levites and priests.

On hearing the comment from the Pharisee, Jesus spoke quietly to Peter and said: "I don't want to debate with these people. Let's go. I will show you a place in Jerusalem that is filled with God's people."

• • •

Jesus led them through the lower part of the city where craftsmen lived with their wives and families in small houses with tiny shops, and then to the garbage dump so they could see and experience the homeless scavenging for food. "I'm starting to catch on Master. This is where you decided the Temple tax could be better used to help the poor," Peter said.

"You, Peter, are a very thoughtful man. That tax and what it goes to support at the Temple are abominations."

"I couldn't agree more," Sarah said. "This whole scene is turning my stomach."

"Wait till you see the mansions of the rich," Jesus said.

"I have seen enough of Jerusalem my good friends," Peter said. "Someone, please, lead us back to the warm home of Lazarus and his sisters."

"I think you have a good idea, Peter. Seeing all those rich homes will do nothing but make us all mad." The five traveling companions headed back to Bethany. An hour later, as the time approached the ninth hour, they came upon the home of Lazarus. Martha came running toward them as soon as they came over the rise and into view.

"Master, come quickly," Martha yelled out when she was fifty yards from them. "My brother is dead."

A Man Called Jesus • 97

"Lazarus is dead?" John said. "How can that be? We left here only this morning, and he wished us all a good trip."

"What do you mean your brother is dead? What happened?" Jesus asked as Martha came up to them. Jesus moved toward her to embrace her. She immediately broke out into uncontrollable tears. After regaining some of her composure, she responded.

"It happened right after you left. He just collapsed in the courtyard. Thank heavens Judas and Philip were still here. They carried our dear brother to his bed."

"But how do you know he is dead?" Jesus persisted.

"Because he doesn't seem to be breathing. When they first placed him on the bed, he was breathing a little, but that seems to have stopped. Please come quickly and see for yourself." Jesus entered the house and went directly to Lazarus's room. The family left the two of them alone. Jesus looked at Lazarus who was lying on his bed with his eyes closed facing the wall. Jesus took the hand of his friend and knelt down beside the bed.

"Lazarus, my dear friend, you can't be dead. You can't die on me. Yahweh, you must not let me lose my friend." He continued holding his hand, kneeling there beside him. Lazarus did not move. The sun grew dim, and Jesus remained there holding his hand. Mary poked her head in and brought Jesus a small wooden chair for him to sit on. Jesus sat on the chair, rubbed his knees, and continued holding Lazarus's hand.

He nodded off to sleep. When he awoke, it was pitch dark, and there was a blanket drooped over his shoulder. He struggled in his mind to orient himself, to put it all together. Mary must have come back. I must have nodded off again. He was still holding Lazarus's hand, and for some strange reason the hand felt warmer. His heart filled with joy. "Yahweh be praised," he mumbled as he looked toward the ceiling. And then doubts swept through him. Was the hand really warmer? Although he could not see Lazarus, he sensed that he had not moved. He could not hear him breathing. "Yahweh, please don't take my friend from me," he called out silently into the night. He kept holding Lazarus's hand.

An hour later Martha came in to check on him. Jesus's head jerked downward, and he abruptly awakened. I dozed off again, he reflected.

"Martha," Jesus whispered up at her as he gained his wits about him. "Here. Take Lazarus's hand. It seems warmer to me. What do you think?" She took the hand of her brother, and then gave it back to Jesus. She then stepped closer to the bed and placed her hand on her brother's chest. A moment later she whispered to Jesus in excitement.

"I feel a slight movement in his chest. You have brought him back to us Master. Yahweh be praised."

"I think it's a little early to say that, but I will keep holding his hand. I will pray to God that he bring him back to us."

"Call me, Master, if there is any change. I will be in the main room praying with my sister."

Two hours later Lazarus wakened Jesus when he spoke in a quiet, soft voice to his friend. "Is that you, Master, holding my hand? How long have I been asleep?"

"Oh Lazarus, my Lazarus. You have come back to us. May God be praised." Three days later Jesus and his group of eleven fellow travelers left Bethany to return to their homes in Galilee. Lazarus was there to say goodbye to them at the door.

"My good friends from Galilee you have given me a new field. We thank you for that. Jesus, my Master and dearest friend in this world, you have given me back my life. May Yahweh be praised. You both speak and act for him, my Jesus. God speed to all of you on your journey home, and please return in haste." Jesus waved to his friend and fought back tears. The Galileans left with a full heart and many, many questions. They would talk among themselves for the next four days. The residents of Bethany would have similar conversations.

Notes

1. The month of Kislev on the Hebrew calendar spans from late November to late December.
2. Psalms made up a large part of the hymnal for Jews living at the time of Jesus. See Psalm 33.
3. See Explanatory Notes for a further discussion of John the Baptist.

4. Jewish males and females were allowed in the Women's Court. Only Jewish males were allowed in the Court of Israel.

5. The Sanhedrin was the highest religious, political, and judicial authority in Israel.

6. Numbers 6:24-26.

7. Hosea 6:6.

8. Leviticus 11: 9-12.

9. Leviticus 19:18.

10. This story is taken from Luke 10: 29-37.

## 9: HONORING THE SABBATH AS GOD INTENDED

It was the 18th day of Adar[1], and Jesus was on his way to Mount Tabor.[2] Mount Tabor is located in lower Galilee on the eastern end of the Jezreel Valley, a two hour walk from Nazareth. The mountain rises 1,900 feet from the flat terrain surrounding it.

Jesus was joined by Alphie and Aaron, his two closest childhood friends. It was the sabbath and early spring, and Jesus was looking forward to celebrating both. He also wanted to thank his two friends for loaning their donkeys for the recent trip to Jerusalem. They set out a little after the noon meal with plans to spend the night on the summit.

"I'm surprised Rebecca let you come with us, Alphie," Aaron said as they left through the village gate and headed east along a well-traveled path that would take them to the base of the mountain.

"She and Tamar are spending the afternoon with their mother. They don't need me around. She likes me palling with Jesus. Makes me a better person she says," and he slapped Jesus on the shoulder. "Do you think he deserves all that credit, old buddy?" he said as he looked across at Aaron.

"Women can say that because they played quoits with him,"[3] Aaron responded with a smile.

"We all played together," Jesus protested.

"Yes, because you would give the ball to the girls so they could play. Without you, they never would have captured the ball. That must be where Rebecca is coming from. I remember her hanging around with us and trying to play."

"We do go back a long way," Jesus said.

"Do you remember when I asked my parents to negotiate a marriage contract with her family?"

"We were about fourteen," Jesus replied.

"I named this mountain for her then."

"Mount Rebecca? Why?" asked Aaron.

"Because it looks like a woman's breast. Have you not eyes to see."

"You had seen nothing at fourteen," Aaron promptly replied.

"Imagination. A year later I discovered how right I was."

"I love these fields of our neighbor Jacob."

"You always change the conversation Jesus when things get good," Alphie protested.

"But look at all the wildflowers. They are just coming into bloom."

"I would rather talk about Rebecca coming into bloom," Alphie responded with a laugh.

"You were lucky with her, Alphie," Aaron chimed in. "She's a good woman."

"I know. Remember Thaddeus, Jesus, the mason we worked with on the theater in Sepphoris?"

"Sure. He's a fine fellow. How's he doing?"

"Not too well. His wife has leprosy, and she was forced to leave her village. Maybe you should go see her."

"Where does she live?"

"I'm not sure. I'll find out from Thaddeus next time I see him."

"I'm not exactly sure what I can do for her."

"She should be easy after that guy Lazarus," Alphie said as he again slapped Jesus on the shoulder. "Everyone is talking about it."

"It's so strange, Alphie. God seems to be working through me in some way."

"Keep the emphasis on strange. You always defined God as mystery Jesus."

"If I really have these powers, I hope I use them only to do good."

"Alphie just reminded me of your helping girls. The only problem I had with you as a kid is that you always seemed to be that way. I remember telling my sister I would give you a denarius if you ever said something bad about someone."

"Thanks, Aaron. I certainly remember some bad things, but I guess it's good you didn't notice."

"Speaking of bad things, rumor has it you saw a lot of bad things in Jerusalem," Alphie said.

"In many ways, it was a real disappointment."

"What did you find so disturbing? I've often thought I should take my family to one of the festivals," Aaron continued.

"I wouldn't waste your time," Alphie chimed in. "James found the sacrifices to be disgusting."

"James is right about that. I just don't understand how sacrificing an animal can lead to the forgiveness of sin. It's like we're trying to bribe God."

"The trip is expensive too," Alphie said.

"It certainly can be," Jesus replied.

"What about the city itself?" Aaron asked.

"It makes Sepphoris look like a village with its huge palaces, fancy gardens, and pools for cooling off in the hot summer."

"Thanks to all the taxes they squeeze out of us," Alphie said.

"My friend Judas from Capernaum made the same point."

"You know, we just finished speaking of God as a mystery," Aaron said. "Here's a mystery I can't figure out. I was taught as a kid that riches are a sign of God's blessing, and yet rich people can often be so unkind. Just take our buddy here. The drought three years ago about ruined your family Alphie. Your brother had to take out a large loan from some rich Jew in Sepphoris so you could plant a new wheat crop."

"We pay the robber twenty-five percent on that loan. If I'm not mistaken Yahweh forbids the charging of interest."

"You are right about that. It's right in Exodus,"[4] Jesus said. "That rich Jew that God blesses has forced you to work as a day laborer in Sepphoris to help repay the loan."

"That's what happens to the third son.[5] I hate it."

"I've been thinking about this problem a lot recently, and have concluded that what we learned as children may not be right. God may think quite differently. Where does the teaching about wealth as a sign of blessing come from? It comes from the Temple priests in Jerusalem, the ones with the huge palaces. No one asks us poor people what God thinks. So ask this poor guy what God thinks about wealth and blessing Aaron."

"What does God think about wealth and blessing, Jesus?"

"That the last shall be first. When God brings us his kingdom, we will be its first citizens."

"I hope you are right about that my favorite teacher and childhood friend. Now listen guys. We're getting near to the base of the mountain, and there's little wood to be had on top. We'll want a fire tonight so we better collect some wood while we can still find it on the ground," Aaron said as he left the path and walked into the woods on his left to begin the search for wood.

"Use your imagination guys and think of my Rebecca. She's as smooth as that dome up there. That's why Aaron's right. We better get the wood here before we reach that dome."

• • •

"Aaron, I have a question for you," Jesus said as he smiled across at his friend. "It relates to an issue that has bothered me since my first trip to Jerusalem." The three friends were sitting around a small fire at the summit of Mount Tabor. They had enjoyed an evening meal of flat bread, cheese, and salted fish from a catch Jesus's nephew, Benjamin, had made a few days ago. Benjamin, James's eleven- year old son, had become quite a fisherman. The stars were shinning, and the three friends were sipping wine.

"Fire away," Aaron replied returning Jesus's smile.

"Who was your father?"

"Why do you ask? That's a really dumb question for you to ask," Aaron responded with a note of tension in his voice.

"You'll see in a minute. I mean no harm by the question."

"My mother has tried to keep this a family secret, but everyone knows by now I'm sure. To answer your question, it was some Roman soldier who forced her to live with him when she was fourteen."

"As you so well know, my story is the same. Do you know what this would mean if we lived in Jerusalem? Neither you or I could marry a

Jewish girl. I would not have been allowed to marry my Anna. My choices would have been limited to a Gentile, a girl of mixed blood or a slave. You and I would have been looked down upon as someone who is polluted."

"You just made my decision about Jerusalem for me. I'm not going to a festival."

"Good decision, although you would probably sell a lot of jewelry there," Alphie piped in.

"I've got two questions that relate to all of this," Jesus said.

"Oh boy, here we go," Alphie responded with a laugh. "Jesus has another big issue for us to debate."

"You can go to bed my good friend."

"No, no. This ought to be good, but I've got to pee first. I'll take a little trip and be back in a minute. But don't wait for me."

"Are you wondering about whether God cares about our ethnic origin?" Aaron asked as Alphie stepped away from the fire and into the night.

"Yes, that's one of my questions. You and I had no control over who we would get for parents. Is it fair to punish us for something that is no fault of ours?"

"I've never felt punished because I had a Gentile father."

"Good point, but save it. You are getting to my second question. Regarding our origin, no God of love would discriminate against us for something totally beyond our control. You and I can't be priests or Levites."

"Who wants to be?" Alphie blurted out as he returned to his place around the fire.

"That's not the point. You can become a priest, but Aaron and I can't because of our birth."

"God help Judaism if I ever become a priest," Alphie said with the belly laugh that Jesus has loved since they were kids.

"I think I see what you're getting at Jesus," Aaron said. "A just God would not operate in that way."

"And Yahweh is a just God. It didn't seem to bother Yahweh when Ruth, a Moabite, married Boaz, a Jew. God tells us in Leviticus to treat resident aliens as if they were native born and to love them as ourselves.[6] But, let's move on. I have a question for Alphie to answer."

"I've had a lot of wine, boys. I don't know."

"Why are Nazareth and Jerusalem so different? Why was I able to marry Anna here, but Jerusalem society would not have permitted it? Aaron said while you were off peeing that he had never felt punished because of his Roman father. Why is that?"

"Those are easy questions. I was expecting something so much harder."

"Okay, what is your answer?"

"I have known you and Aaron since we were little boys. We fished together, taunted girls together, played quoits until we shredded that feather stuffed ball our parents made for us. The three of us were like brothers. Why would I look down on my two brothers?"

"That's the answer I was looking for Alphie. Would you like to become my assistant?"

"Do you pay your assistants? Rebecca is demanding in that way."

"Your answer is right on target. You only know God's will when you are relating to people in loving ways. When you make rules for people you don't know in a loving way and say those rules come from God, you are sadly mistaken. You are speaking for God in a way that is totally dishonest. The rules about racial purity were not made by God. Only men make rules that control people in meanspirited ways."

"Man, you're willing to challenge everything. Go for it my adopted brother."

"Nice, Jesus. I couldn't agree more with Alphie. If you don't mind, though, I have a related mystery question to ask you about. Why does God allow the Romans to oppress us? The prophets say it is because we have sinned. Just like I told you I have never felt punished because of who my father was. I also don't feel consumed by sin. Sure, I do things from time-to-time that God might not like."

"Like looking at girls despite being married to Hannah."

"I'm a male, Alphie. What can God expect? He made me this way."

"That's why I love you buddy."

"Your question is a good one, Aaron. The prophet Daniel helped me with this. The prophet's point is that God is just and is not responsible for the Romans being here. Satan is. The Romans are agents of Satan. Evil is real. Its forces are all around us.

"The question now becomes how are we going to defeat it. Many call for a messiah to wage war on the Romans. We have tried that throughout our history, and you and I have Roman fathers because of it. The violent approach has led to one disaster after another.

"God's way is to love. That is how you defeat evil. You start in a little village like Nazareth. When you love your neighbor and work to improve the lives of those around you, you take the sting out of evil. You defeat it. You also encourage God to intervene in some way to speed this process."

"I've got to tell you something, boys. All this talk about love is making me horny. I've either got to go find Rebecca or go to sleep under all these stars."

"I think I'm ready for sleep too, but thank you, Jesus, my friend. I'll think about your answer, and try to do a better job loving and helping my neighbors."

"That's all God asks of you."

"What does God ask of me? I hope not much."

"Only that you continue to honor Mount Rebecca," Aaron said as he got up from the fire.

"I can't keep my hands off of that blessed mountain. I like a God who makes easy demands."

"God loves you, Alphie, and I do too," Jesus said as he got up from the fire to hug his friend. He then went to find his haversack, removed the blanket his sister Naomi had loaned him, and found a soft spot covered with moss to bed down for the night. He lay on his back gazing at the stars and thanking Yahweh for the gift of friendship. Eventually the stars put on a show. They were traveling across the sky leaving a trail of light. Satan can't do that Jesus concluded with a smile. He can't make the stars dance. He can't make the wildflowers bloom in the spring. You can sleep well my Aaron. Love is going to win, and with that thought Jesus closed his eyes and entered into a deep sleep.

• • •

The three companions left as the sun was rising. Aaron was anxious to get back to his blacksmith shop because he had promised to make his cousin Samuel a blade for his plow. Alphie, with a day-off from Sepphoris, had promised Rebecca he would add space to their vegetable garden. The only one without an obligation was Jesus who was confident his family would find something for him to do.

The trip down the mountain went quickly with the three travelers keeping mostly to themselves. As they were about to enter a small wooded area near the base of the mountain, out of nowhere, four young men leaped in front of them with knives drawn. "Stop, all three of you in the name of Yahweh, the real owner of all the land in Israel. My name is Simon ben Joseph, and you are trespassing on land we watch over for our God."

"These guys are bandits," Alphie whispered across to Aaron. "I've heard of this guy. He's from Japha."[7]

"Quiet you with the burly beard," Simon spat out in a voice of disdain. Jesus quickly stepped forward with a large smile on his face.

"My name is Jesus of Nazareth. What can we do for you?"

"Simon, I know your cousin Nicolos. We have worked together in Sepphoris," Alphie said as he moved forward to join Jesus.

"Nicolos is back at our camp."

"Listen, Simon. I have the same problems you do," Alphie continued. "Put those knives away, and we can talk about our common problems."

"How do I know you can be trusted?"

"Go get Nicolos. He will remember me. I loaned him five denarius to help pay his land tax."

"Simon, I think they can be trusted."

"Get Nicolos, Benjamin."

"There's a nice shaded area off to the left. My friends and I would enjoy a short break from our travels. Let's go sit by those trees and talk," Jesus said. Simon and his two remaining companions put their knives away and accepted Jesus's offer.

"Do I know you, Jesus of Nazareth?" Simon asked when they all were seated.

"I have been to Japha a few times in the last six months. Alphie tells us that is where you are from. My brother James has also traveled there."

"We haven't returned to our village recently; but the last time we were there, everyone was talking about some teacher from Nazareth. Is that you?"

"I suppose so."

"What are you teaching? What is your message? I hope it is to kill Romans and their traitor collaborators, the rich Jews."

"Actually my message is quite the opposite. I know you have lost your land through no fault of your own."

"Tell him about it, Bartholomew," Simon barked out like an officer ordering troops.

"My family lost our farm that goes back five generations. It happened last winter when this banker from Sepphoris foreclosed on us."

"They were ruined by the drought too," Alphie said quietly to Aaron.

"Have you also lost your land?" The young man asked in a quiet voice of concern.

"We came close. My brother had to sell his daughter as a slave to this rich Jew in Sepphoris to help repay the loan. She turns twelve next year so she will be coming home soon. I work in Sepphoris. Oh hi, Nicolos. I didn't see you arrive."

"I owe you five denarius."

"Think of it as a sabbatical year."[8]

"God blesses you Alphie," Jesus said.

"How come only us poor people honor God's law concerning the sabbatical year?" Simon blurted out in a voice of disgust. "Finish your story Bartholomew. The good teacher from Nazareth needs to hear it."

"My father took a knife to himself for all the shame of losing our property. It forced my mother to become a cook in Sepphoris and to whore on the side so that she could feed us. I became a camel driver when work was available. When my cousin Nicolos told me about my mother whoring, I joined up with Simon. I feed my family now."

"My name is Thomas, Jesus. We have all lost our land in one way or another."

"That is so unfair," Jesus responded in a soft voice oozing in compassion. "How do you feed your family Bartholomew?"

"By stealing from rich merchants in Sepphoris."

"We are thinking of changing our operation to Gabara,"[9] Thomas interjected, "as a safety precaution. Romans soldiers are out looking for us."

"Thomas, silence that loose tongue," Simon barked out at him. "I'm still not sure these men can be trusted?"

"Your plans are safe with us," Jesus responded in a calm, reassuring voice. "You steal only because you have been stolen from. I don't know how God will sort all of that out, but the fact that you saved your mother from serving the needs of wealthy men warms my heart. Am I right in my assumption, Bartholomew?"

"Yes, but she still cooks in Sepphoris."

"I want to attack the archives in that main administration building and burn all the debt records," Nicolos interjected. Simon's scowl shot daggers. If Nicolos had intended to continue along these lines, he rapidly changed his mind.

"My two companions have a busy day before them so we best be on our way, but I do have two requests to make. First, as your family finances improve, please return to your village. I assume most if not all of you are not married. A good woman is one of God's greatest gifts. The mutual love you share is the best way I know to learn of God's love. It will help you become a better person. My second request is to avoid violence if at all possible when you make your attack. Killing an innocent person is one sin Yahweh has a hard time forgiving."

• • •

Two weeks later Jesus and a group of his close followers were sharing an evening meal at the home of Peter and Sapphua in Capernaum. The atmosphere surrounding the meal was more businesslike than the usual festive tone of these occasions because they were accessing the progress of their movement. Peter, the Zebedee brothers, and Philip were concentrating on the villages north of Capernaum and reported much progress in Bethsaida and Chorazin.

"James and I have made trips to Nain, Japha, and some of the other villages around Sepphoris," Jesus reported.

"Is it time to branch out to villages on the east bank of the Jordan River Master?"

"Let's wait a little on that Judas. There are so many villages in our immediate surroundings we have yet to visit. On another matter, I am happy to report to you one of the best things that has happened to us. All this travel has led to expenses. Mary's brother, Joachim, has promised to help us with our money problems. He owns a fish-salting factory in Magdala. I met him on a recent trip there. Mary once told me that Joachim will be among the first citizens in God's kingdom. She was surely right about that."

"Here's to Joachim," Peter said as he raised his wine glass. "May God's kingdom come so that we can all join him there. It's also nice to know that our fish are going to such a fine man."

"It's my brother's honor to help," Mary said after lowering her wine glass. "It has given him a new purpose in life. Joachim and his family often spend sabbath on this beautiful meadow on the Sea of Galilee between here and Magdala. Let's pack a picnic lunch and take sabbath there tomorrow. If we are lucky, Joachim will be there and you can thank him in person."

Most of those present at Peter's house the night before left at the third hour for the fifty-minute walk to the meadow on the cliff along the shore of the Sea of Galilee. Though it was a beautiful day for such an excursion, Mary, upon arriving, became disappointed for two reasons. First, Joachim was nowhere in sight. In addition, the meadow was crowded with people. It didn't take them long to find Jesus and to pepper him with questions. Mary had hoped for a more private, quiet sabbath.

"Good teacher," one woman addressed Jesus as she approached him sitting on the lush grass surrounded by his friends. "When is the messiah due to arrive?"

"Why do you assume God will send a messiah?"

"Because that is what the prophets tell us."

"Not all of them," Jesus responded. "My favorite prophet Isaiah has a different message. He teaches us that God will bring in his kingdom. Isaiah's point is that only God can be king."[10]

"How will we defeat the Romans then?"

"I get that question all the time, and I have a simple answer. Not by violence. Several of our countrymen have claimed to be messiahs, and their actions have led to disaster. Do you see the lush grass I am sitting on? God brought the rain to make that possible. The wildflowers are in bloom all around us. Any God that can create such beauty will find a way to deal with Rome. So be patient my friend. God will find a way to honor his promises. While we wait, let me suggest a prayer for you to repeat.

"Our Father in heaven,
may your name be held holy,
your kingdom come, your will be done
on earth as it is in heaven.
Give us this day our daily bread.
And forgive us our debts
as we forgive those who are in debt to us.[11]

"Please note my friend that no messiah is mentioned when we ask God to bring in his kingdom. Pray it each night as you go to bed. Your prayer may stimulate God to act."

"You are just like what everyone says. Too good to be true," and she walked away in disgust. Judas followed after her to try to make peace and to maybe change her mind. Jesus just smiled and consoled Mary with the same advice.

"Be patient. Your brother may yet appear." It didn't take long before others came with their questions. Twenty-five or thirty people had gathered around Jesus.

One young man whose wife and three kids stood beside him, asked, "Master, what will this kingdom of God look like?"

"Much like those three beautiful children standing beside you." The man grinned from ear to ear. "But I suppose you would like a few more details."

The man smiled again and said: "No that's okay. I get it."

"In case our kids become naughty, I would like a few details," the young wife interjected, also with a smile.

"Look out at the lake. Do you see the outline of Tiberias?[12] I can see Antipas's new palace and the courthouse he recently created nearby. I can guarantee you the kingdom of God will not look like that. What do we know about large buildings? The simple truth is that they can be destroyed. The kingdom of God is about what is eternal, about what can never be destroyed. Love is your answer. That is what can never be destroyed. In God's kingdom, love will rule."

"Nice answer," a woman toward the back of the crowd blurted out, "but my children can be naughty too. A few more details please. How might a kingdom of God's love affect my life?"

"About a month ago two priests from Sepphoris came to Nazareth on the sabbath and found my brother Joses helping our neighbor Reuben repair his roof. They condemned both men for working on the sabbath.

"The rules governing the sabbath are found in the Torah given to us by Moses.[13] In God's kingdom, the Torah will be enforced with love. When God becomes king, Joses will be honored for helping his neighbor on sabbath day.

"In the prayer I gave to that first woman who no longer seems to be with us, God asks us to forgive those who are in debt to us. Again, in the Torah God gave to Moses, there is a program that will end poverty. God calls on us to forgive those in debt to us every seven years,[14] and he commands that land be returned to its original, ancestral owner every fifty years.[15] These provisions are about economic justice. You can count on those laws being enforced with compassion in God's kingdom."

"What about Gentiles?" a man next to Jesus asked quietly. Will they be included in God's kingdom?"

"Did everyone hear that question? It is a good one. This man beside me wants to know if Gentiles will be included in God's kingdom? As you all know, Galilee has an interesting ethnic mix. We live among Phoenicians, Syrians, Arabs, and Greeks. We are very different from Judea in this sense. Our scriptures tell us that God's promises pertain to the people of Israel which implies that his kingdom will be for the people of Israel, for Jews.

"But you must always remember that this will be a kingdom where love rules. One important aspect of love is that it is inclusive. This means that Phoenicians, Syrians, Arabs, and Greeks are our neighbors, which God will demand we both include in his new society and love as our own. This applies to Samaritans, mixed race Jews, lepers, and all those others who are currently seen as a blemish to society. In God's kingdom, the last shall be first, those seen as having a blemish will be loved and included.

"You know all this talk has made me hungry. I will be happy to answer other questions while we eat. I see that many of you brought blankets. Let's spread out a few of these blankets on the ground, and we can all place the food we brought for the mid-day meal on them. I can think of no better way to celebrate the sabbath then by sharing a meal together."

Notes

1. March.
2. Christian tradition places the transfiguration there.
3. A game where the ball is thrown in the air which children try to catch—an ancient version of keep away.
4. Exodus 22: 25.
5. Deuteronomy 21: 17 commands that the oldest son receive a double inheritance. For one third in line, that often meant becoming a day laborer.
6. Leviticus 19: 34.
7. A small village a mile and a half from Nazareth.
8. God commands in Deuteronomy 15:2 that every seventh year be declared a sabbatical year in which all debts are forgiven.
9. Gabara was an important administrative center ten miles from Sepphoris.
10. See Isaiah 43: 15, 44: 6 and 52:7.
11. Matthew 6: 9-12.
12. Antipas moved the capital of Galilee from Sepphoris to Tiberias in 19 CE.
13. Exodus 23: 12.
14. Deuteronomy 15: 1-2.
15. Leviticus 25: 8-12.

## 10: WHO AM I?

It was a beautiful, late fall day, and Mary set off from Magdala with a satchel full of coins to deliver to Judas, the movement's treasurer. She got a late start and hoped the light would last long enough for her to reach Capernaum. She arrived at Peter's house in the middle of the evening meal. The group was in the midst of having a meeting. The dinner hadn't been planned that way, but Judas kept raising the issue of Jesus's identity. He believed he was a prophet, and was frustrated Jesus was not acting like one.

The meal was fish stew that was made under the supervision of Sapphua, Peter's wife, though each family contributed. In addition, there was plenty of bread and plenty of wine. The latter added to the boisterous atmosphere around the table and may have loosened some lips.

"Judas, we talk about the Master's identity all the time," Peter said as he shoved his bowl aside and filled his wine glass once again. "You think he's a prophet, and I'm beginning to think he's more than that."

"The problem is not whether he's a prophet. He surely is," Judas replied. "He speaks with prophetic authority. He teaches with that same authority. He attracts large crowds."

"He's a beautiful, beautiful man," Mary said as a deep smile crossed her face.

"That he is, no doubt," Judas responded. "But let's get back to the central issue here. He doesn't act like a prophet. Prophets perform symbolic acts of protest to dramatize their message. Hosea married a whore to make his point.[1] People remembered that act."

"When prophets take actions, it often challenges God to act," John said.

"So what do you want Jesus to do?" Peter asked. "Take some symbolic act that people remember? Burn down a customs house or lay himself down in front of Roman troops?"

"That would certainly help," Judas said. "It might get God to intervene as John so rightly pointed out."

"Maybe God has already intervened?" Peter said.

"What do you mean by that?" Judas responded.

"I think Jesus may be the messiah. If so, God has intervened. Jesus is here. The prophet Daniel teaches us that Satan was responsible for the evil in the world. This evil takes residence in humans in the form of demons or disease. Don't you see that Jesus is defeating this evil. It's a huge battle, and Jesus is winning."

"I agree with Peter," Mary said. "He defeated the demons inside me. Philip brought Thaddeus from Bethsaida to see Jesus. Now his demons are gone, defeated. And then there's Rachel. I'm not sure, but she may have been demon possessed. If so, they're gone now. Mine have disappeared. I am a new person because of this wonderful man. Sarah told me about this leper from Cana that Jesus healed."

"We heard from James that Jesus cured some poor guy with leprosy in Nain," Andrew interjected.

"How much evidence do we need?" Mary continued.

"Don't forget Lazarus," Peter bellowed out. "That's the big one. Our Master brought him back to life. I still can't believe it. The prophet Isaiah says these things happen when the messiah has come. Jesus is out there defeating evil. The kingdom of God is coming. Jesus is defeating the forces of Satan to allow this great event to happen.[2] And here's the best part. Our wonderful leader, bless his heart, seems to have no idea about the role he is playing."

"Every time someone asks him about a messiah, he claims there won't be one, that God will act on his own," Philip said.

"The fact that he's the messiah doesn't mean he can't be wrong about a few things," Peter quickly responded. "Sometimes his humility gets in the way of his ability to put all the facts together."

"That's the whole point," Judas said. "You may be right that he is the messiah, but he must act. He must come to understand his role so that he will act. Once he acts, God will surely intervene."

"I'll tell you one thing he will never do," John of Zebedee shouted out. "He will never call on us to take up arms. He keeps saying that God will find his own way to push out Rome."

"Let's get back to his being a prophet," Judas said. "I agree with you that he will never be, for lack of a better word, your normal messiah. So let's get him to act more like a prophet. I'm beginning to think we should encourage him to perform some great symbolic act."

"Like what?" Peter intoned.

"For me, the most natural target is the Temple," Judas said. "Ritual abuse, the squandering of so much money, the idea that God is so petty and small he requires us to atone for our sins, the corrupt High Priest and his legions of functionaries; these are all issues Jesus comes back to time and time again. I don't think he believes Yahweh actually resides in the Temple. He keeps telling us the best place to find God is here, at our common meals."

"So you want him to attack the Temple," Philip said.

"Not physically," Judas responded, "but symbolically. I was thinking he could free all the animals. That would be a symbolic act that tells people in a graphic way the sacrifice system is an abomination."

"Freeing the animals. I bet James would help him do that," Peter speculated as he poured himself another glass of wine. Sapphua got up from the table and took the wine jug with her. Peter smiled and shook his head.

"Would that get him into trouble?" Mary asked.

"Not with the Romans," Peter replied. "The Romans could care less about our sacrifice system. Our Jews wouldn't be much of a problem either. What could that overstuffed High Priest do? The only thing would be to order Jesus to purchase some innocent ram and then beg for God's forgiveness. And do you know what? There would be no ram to purchase. They will have all fled the Temple."

"Where would the animals go?" Mary asked.

"I guess they would wander around Jerusalem," Andrew said.

"So who's going to tell Jesus about this plan?" Peter inquired.

"I think we should raise the issue with James. He's Jesus's brother, and I know from our discussions he hates the sacrifice system," Judas said.

"You have really thought this out, my friend," Peter said. "I'm impressed. I will find some way to raise the issue with James. A nice symbolic act. I think James will love the idea."

"If that's what you want to do, we should probably do it at Passover, although I certainly don't want to go back to Jerusalem any time soon," John said. "Passover is all about atonement and sacrifice. Jesus freeing the animals then would certainly get everyone's attention."

"I think we have a plan," Peter said.

• • •

Three weeks later James took a walk with his brother.

"Why all the secrecy, James? Why didn't Peter come to me directly?"

"I guess because he thought you would have more difficulty saying no to me."

"This puts it right on the line for me. Who am I? What does God want me to do?"

"It is clear you have some special function, and we need to figure it out. Let's go over here by this pretty stream and sit. I'm a little tired from all that clearing this morning. The winter is a good time to clear fields, but it is hard work. That sparkling water over there will refresh us."

After sitting and reflecting some, Jesus looked directly at his brother. "I think of myself as a teacher, James, and I know there are people who call me a prophet. There's a huge difference between the two vocations. A teacher is a role you choose. To become a prophet, you must be chosen by God."

"You are right about that distinction," James said smiling over at his brother. "Now think about Lazarus. Think about Susanna, that leper you healed who was living in a cave outside of Nain."

"I do, brother, all the time. That is what is so confusing."

"God must be working through you, Jesus. Lazarus is alive. God worked through you to bring him back to life. I certainly couldn't have done that. You are much more than a teacher, my good brother." Jesus embraced him.

"You may be right," Jesus said after resuming his position on the rock. "I reach out to people and things happen. All I want to do is teach about God's love. I'm scared, James."

"I would be too, but don't forget one thing. If God has given you this power, it is his power. He will see that you do the right thing. You know, my brother, so many of our prophets were reluctant to do God's work. Just think of Jeremiah."

"I have thought about Jeremiah. Rachel made the same point. But your point is helpful. If God has given me this power, I need not worry. He will make sure I do the right thing."

"I think so, my brother. Now back to the meeting with Peter. Judas's point is that of course you are a prophet, and the time has come for you to start acting like one."

"That Judas is certainly one diamond in the rough."

"He has an edge to him, but he is loyal with a sharp mind for getting things done."

"What does he want me to do?"

"Some symbolic act of protest. Some act that people will remember. Some act that defines your message. Judas wants all of Israel to know you. He wants you to directly challenge our Temple-based religion."

"Dear God, that's a tall order."

"He wants you to go to Jerusalem and free all those animals in the Court of Gentiles. I would add the moneychangers. They symbolize all the corruption and greed. That recent trip to Jerusalem was eye opening for me. The God of love you bring to me every day I'm in your presence must find that whole Temple scene an abomination."

"So you're with Judas in devising this strategy?"

"Why do you say that?"

"Because you want to add the moneychangers."

"I think Judas is making a good point. He has no fear you will be arrested. The Romans could care less about the sacrifice system, Judas says. Or maybe it was Peter who made that point. He's one hundred percent behind this plan, too."

"I'm not afraid of Rome either. When does he want us to take action?"

"He's not talking about us, Jesus. He's talking about you. You are the prophet. Prophets are not like military leaders. They don't lead people into battle. They speak the word of God and act out that word alone. I would love to free all those animals, but God has not called me to make that symbolic statement. He has called you."

"I'm back to thinking this thing is a tall order."

"I know. Maybe you should give it a little time. Think about it a bit."

"No, James. I'm ready. I concluded I was called by God to perform some special function in that dream I had returning from Jerusalem. I can't ignore the fact that I affect people."

"All for the good," James interjected.

"That seems to be true."

"If you are affecting people for the good, God must be working through you."

"I was coming to that conclusion on my own, but you have helped me clarify things. When does Judas want me to act?"

"The Capernaum group was thinking Passover would be a good time. There are thousands of people there, and the focus of the celebration is sacrifice and atonement."

"I also want to somehow make the point about where God lives. I certainly don't find him in that Temple."

"Maybe you should break into the Holy of Holies and tell people it's all a fraud."

"That would certainly get the attention of Caiaphas, but I will start with the animals first."

"Don't forget the moneychangers," James said as he got up from the rock. He was thinking it was time for him to get back to work.

"What should I do about them?" Jesus asked as he, too, got up from the rock.

"I would upset their tables and scatter all those coins."

"You guys have planned this whole thing well. Now let me go back and get some tools so I can help you with that field."

"That proves it, brother," James said with a wide grin. "You are a prophet indeed. You have read my mind. I was hoping you would help me with that field."

Notes

1. Hosea married a whore to demonstrate the unfaithfulness of the people of Israel to their God.
2. See discussion of the miracles in the Explanatory Notes.

## 11: A Good Plan Fails

The Galileans left for Jerusalem fifteen months after their last journey as the cock crowed on the ninth day of Nisan.[1] The timing of this trip was important as Nathanael explained in his history lesson, which was given at Peter's house a month earlier. "Passover is the celebration of the people of Israel's delivery from slavery in Egypt, as I'm sure you all know. When the Pharaoh freed them after a series of tense negotiations with Moses, the Israelites left in such a hurry they could not wait for the dough in their bread to rise—the leaven. As a result, no leavened bread is to be eaten during Passover."

"So that's where it comes from," Rebecca, the wife of Philip said. "I've always wondered about that."

"The celebration is often referred to as the Feast of Unleaven Bread," Nathanael said while smiling at Rebecca. "But here is where the timing of our trip is important. Every family, who can afford it, purchases an animal to sacrifice at the Temple on the afternoon of the fourteenth of Nisan. They eat what remains of the animal the next evening on the fifteenth. So the best time for Jesus to make the protest would be in the late afternoon of the fourteenth when people are purchasing animals. If we leave on the ninth, we should be in Bethany at mid-day on the thirteenth."

The trip was different in two ways from the first one. First, most of the members of Jesus's family tagged along. Mary, the mother of Jesus, had encouraged them. She was coming because she was worried about this protest and because she wanted to meet Lazarus. With the number of travelers at twenty, Jesus was a little concerned they would overwhelm Rachel and Lazarus.

The other big difference became manifest when they arrived in Askar at dusk on the second day, and there was no Rachel. Jesus was disappointed not to see her and yet excited about the prospect of her being back in the village and living with Jacob. Jesus wished there was some way he could get in touch with her, but a trip into the village did not make sense. In Rachel's absence, her house provided them with an oven to cook dinner and shelter for some of the travelers that night.

The two-day trip from Askar to Bethany was uneventful. Jesus couldn't believe it was the third time he had made the trip within the last two years. As they passed through Jericho, he wondered about Thaddeus the blacksmith and his attractive wife Hannah. It would have been nice to have seen them.

But he didn't miss Lazarus. Looking a little older but still remarkably distinguished and fit, Lazarus ran to greet them from the field adjacent to his barn as the Galileans came upon his thirty-five- acre farm. "Mary and Martha," he yelled out. "We will need five more chickens for dinner. Jesus is back."[2]

Mary, Jesus's mother, was thrilled to meet Lazarus and his two sisters. She had heard so much about them on this trip and before. She couldn't keep her eyes from Lazarus for the first hour after their arrival. "This is the man my son brought back to life," she said to herself. "May God be praised."

The weary Galileans were excited to have finally arrived. Lazarus and his two sisters were excited to have them for the seven days of the Passover celebration. There was one brief incident, however, that dampened, somewhat, this giddy atmosphere of joy. It involved Judas and Lazarus.

"Let me go help you butcher those chickens, Lazarus," Judas said when things had quieted down a little and the Galileans had stowed away their gear.

"I would appreciate that, Judas. Come with me. We'll do it at the barn." On the way there, Judas explained to Lazarus their plans for tomorrow. "Oh, I would be careful. There will be perhaps ten thousand tourists at the Court of Gentiles tomorrow purchasing animals for sacrifice. The Temple Guard will be everywhere. The Romans will be on edge."

"What do Romans care about rituals being performed in a Jewish Temple?"

"It's the Passover ritual, Judas. It commemorates the freeing of Israel from the Egyptians. Most of those ten thousand tourists are waiting for God to free them from the Romans."

"I am one of those people."

"That is why the Romans are on edge. They will put down quickly any disturbance, no matter how small."

"Lazarus, while I do not share your concerns, I do have an important favor to ask. Please don't discuss your concerns with the Master. We have planned his protest carefully, and he is really excited to perform it. This action will bring his message to so many more people. It will make him known throughout Judea."

"I promise not to discuss it with him unless he asks. The one thing I will not do is lie to the man who saved my life."

• • •

After the noon meal the next day, everyone set out for Jerusalem. The one thing Jesus was not was excited. He was nervous and having some second thoughts. Confrontations of this kind were not part of his nature. He silently prayed to Yahweh to free him from this burden. "If you can't do that Yahweh, I know you will help me in my time of need."

His mood lifted considerably as they passed through the Garden of Gethsemane. It was a beautiful spring day, with wild flowers surrounding them and a stream to their left bubbling down from the Mount of Olives. God was good. Life was special. He now knew exactly what he would say in the Court of Gentiles. He felt better about the protest. It was a good thing he did not notice his mother's look of concern as they approached the imposing one hundred foot wall of the Temple. Mary had this vision of a dark, cold prison with these burly, mean-spirited looking guards standing around with swords at their sides. Despite the optimism of her fellow compatriots, she could not shake it.

Once the group had completed their ritual baths and all protesters were inside the Temple grounds, Judas took over. He led them to an open area in the Court of Gentiles near to where the animals were kept. Hundreds of sheep were bleating in their pens. Fifty yards to the right were the tables with the moneychangers. The Temple officials were working frantically to keep up with the rapidly expanding crowd.

When the Galileans were in place, Judas called out in a loud voice: "My fellow worshippers in the great Temple of Yahweh. We are honored this afternoon to have a prophet among us. Come gather around and hear the word of God."

A few curious onlookers approached the Galileans. Jesus gave them time, and when he finally started to speak several others had joined them. "My friends, I have just walked through God's world. The Garden of Gethsemane with its wild flowers, olive orchards, and trickling streams is a wonderful expression of God's wonder, his majesty, his goodness, and his love. I sensed his presence with every step I took.

"And then I entered these Temple grounds. Yahweh disappeared. In his place, I sensed greed, corruption, frantic bargaining with regard to animal prices, and anxiety as worshippers pushed and shoved their way through the ritual baths. Now many of you are worried about whether you can afford an animal for sacrifice." A crowd was gathering around him. He raised his voice.

"The focus of the Passover celebration is the sacrifice of a paschal lamb. You have all come to sacrifice an animal to get right with Yahweh. Have you ever thought about what this ritual says about Yahweh? It makes him into a mean, petty tyrant who needs to be humored with the slaughter of an innocent animal in order to further relate to you.

"My friends, Yahweh is a God of love, a love that is so deep he cannot help but relate to you. You change nothing when you sacrifice an animal. To make God present in your life, love and serve your neighbor. Sure, it is important to avoid sin. You cannot sin and love your neighbor. The good news is that God forgives your sin. He does not require animal sacrifice, only a humble disposition and a renewed commitment to love. God forgives you because he loves you, not because you go into bankruptcy trying to appease him with the slaughter of an innocent animal.

"Fifteen months ago we Galileans were at this Temple for the Feast of Lights. On the first night of the celebration, we watched the High Priest sacrifice an unblemished ram to atone for the sin of some unknown person who stood in the audience with us. That person's only concern was that the odor from the burning meat was pleasing to Yahweh. The priests stood around the altar looking bored with this silly ritual. Can Yahweh be bribed in such a manner? When the service ended, I turned to my brother and recited from Hosea. 'What I want is love, not sacrifice; knowledge of God, not holocausts.'"[3]

"Good teacher, your words are inspiring," Judas called out. He and Jesus had rehearsed this part together. The Hosea citation was the signal. "Now show us what you plan to do about it."

"Watch me," Jesus said, and he turned to run toward the money tables. When he got there, he found eight tables pushed together. He ran his arm across all eight tables scattering the coins every which way. The dealers were taken by surprise. The worshippers were shocked, which led them to move away from the tables quickly. This enabled Jesus to turn over each of the tables. "My house will be called a house of prayer for all the nations. You have made it into a den of thieves," he called out in a loud voice for all to hear.[4]

After finishing with the tables, he ran fifty yards to his right where the animals were kept. He opened stalls and untied ropes. He then opened several layers of stacked pigeon cages as far as he could reach. It didn't take long before hundreds of animals were running around frantically dodging confused and nervous worshippers.

When he was satisfied the job was completed, he quietly walked back to the awestruck Galileans and said: "Let's go home."

• • •

It took Judas a while to catch up with his friends. He had one more errand to do. He went in search of the priest he had seen watching the protest from the second floor balcony dressed in an elaborate white robe with a red sash. He eventually found him in an animated discussion with three of his colleagues at the entrance to the Court of Israel. He tapped the priest's shoulder and said, "Sir, did you witness the demonstration in the Court of Gentiles fifteen minutes ago?"

"That Galilean profaned the Temple. You sound like one too."

"I am from Capernaum, here for my first Passover, but I am not one of them. Because they are fellow Galileans I began talking with one of his followers before the demonstration began. This man they call Jesus is a troublemaker."

"All Galileans are troublemakers," the priest barked back to Judas. "What did you learn?" The priest's three colleagues ended their discussion, and gave their full attention to Judas.

"He wants to destroy the Temple, sir. His protest this afternoon was the first step in his plan of destruction."

"Who is this rabble-rouser from Galilee?"

"The follower I spoke with claims he is a prophet. I got the impression from listening to others in their group that they think of him as the messiah. They call him Jesus of Nazareth."

"They all make such claims. False prophets are a dangerous menace. A pretender messiah is even more dangerous. What do you know about his further plans?"

"Nothing really. When I asked about them, the follower I spoke with merely said: 'watch him.' It's a strange group of followers. I learned that one was a tax collector, and there are several sinners. These people could care less about the Laws of Moses. Oh, I almost forgot. There was a Samaritan woman among them."

"He certainly associates with dangerous people," one of the priests said.

"Well, I just thought I should bring this matter to your attention," Judas said.

"You have served Yahweh well. He says he wants to destroy the Temple, that this afternoon was the first step," the priest mumbled to himself.

"That was what I heard."

"And you said this man goes by the name of Jesus?"

"Yes. That is what I was told, though I was never introduced to him."

"Do you have any idea how we could find him?"

"I understand these Galileans are staying somewhere in Bethany. The man I spoke with said they plan to return to the Temple tomorrow after the noon meal."

"What gate will they use? Did your contact give you any idea about that?"

"They entered through the East Gate this afternoon. I met them right there at the ritual bath."

"That's the best place for someone coming from Bethany to enter," one of the three priests said.

"And you are sure this man wants to destroy God's Temple?" the short, thin, mousy priest asked who had remained silent until now.

"That's what I was led to believe. I just thought someone at the Temple should know about this plot."

"You did the right thing. It's nice to meet a Galilean who is not out to make trouble."

Judas took this last comment to mean his meeting was over. He bowed to the four priests, and then walked rapidly to the marble stairway that would take him to the Court of Gentiles, the first leg of his journey back to Bethany. He was anxious to return to the home of Lazarus before he was missed. Judas was now convinced God would intervene to save his prophet and to inaugurate his kingdom.

• • •

The weary group of protestors arrived at the farm of Lazarus as the sun was setting in the western sky. They were giddy with their success. "Passover Seder will commence as soon as the table is prepared," Lazarus announced in a loud, clear voice as the group made the turn toward his house. "We have a lot to celebrate."[5]

Mary and Martha organized the women for that task. The table was set with the finest silverware and place settings. Wine glasses and a small bowl of salt water were also distributed at each place at the table. A wide variety of vegetables were prepared.[6]

Martha was in charge of getting the matzo bread ready. She was assisted by Rebecca and Mary, the mother of Jesus and James. "The matzo bread is passed around the table two times," Martha said to Rebecca who was unfamiliar with the precise details of the Passover ritual. "The first time it is covered with bitter herbs which symbolizes the harsh conditions our slaves endured in Egypt. Toward the end of the meal the bread is passed again. This time it is covered in charoset, which symbolizes the mortar used by our Jewish slaves in building their storehouses."[7]

"How much wine do we drink?" Sapphua asked as she entered the kitchen to gather plates for the table. "I will have to keep my eye on Peter."

"Four toasts are made to Yahweh," Martha replied. "You can make them all with one glass or with four."

"Oh dear," Sapphua said with a grin. "With Peter you can be sure it will be four." An hour later, with everything prepared, Lazarus welcomed his guests to the table. As the first serving of matzo bread was being passed, he stood from his chair raising his wine glass.

"As the host of the occasion, it is my honor to make the first toast. Before I do that, however, my sister Mary has asked that we forgo the traditional serving of lamb. Our Master," and he smiled across at Jesus, "has given her much to think about with regard to the sacrifice system of our fathers. Yahweh, I hope you will forgive us if we have this wrong." And with that he raised his glass high. After briefly pausing, he continued: "We thank you, Yahweh, for choosing our people to covenant with, and we also thank you for honoring your commitment to protect us from the Egyptians. Happy Seder everyone."

The talk that followed was all about the animals at the Temple. "I wonder where they went?" Rebecca blurted out.

"The more important question is whether the priests were able to round them up," James said. "I imagine them somehow escaping."

"I praise Yahweh that Jesus wasn't arrested," Philip said.

"It happened too quickly," Judas responded. "We caught them by surprise." He then stood up to make the second toast. Raising his wine glass, he said: "Yahweh, we celebrate your great victory over the Egyptians tonight, and look forward to your speedy defeat of the Romans."

James gave the third toast in which he thanked Yahweh for giving the Jews the Law, asking him to open their eyes to the spirit of that Law as his brother had so ably taught them. As the meal drew to a close, Jesus raised his glass for the last toast. His comrades had deliberately left him with that honor.

"Yahweh, let me begin this last toast by thanking our hosts Lazarus, Mary, and Martha. My good friends, you have housed us, fed us, and entertained us. There are no better servants of Yahweh among the Jewish people." Raising his glass, he concluded: "Yahweh, we look forward to you delivering us from the Romans in your own time and in your own way.

"My friends, we made a good start this afternoon with the animals and the moneychangers. Tomorrow afternoon we will set out for Jerusalem, again right after the noon meal. This time we will walk past the Temple and enter the city at the Tower of Siloam. Lazarus will lead us to the garbage dump where the homeless forage for food. Our plan will be to gather together as many homeless people as we can and bring them back to the Temple. We will camp with them on the Temple grounds until the High Priest agrees to feed them and open up his treasury to provide them with housing. So bring what you think you will need for what could be a long stay.

"Again, thank you Lazarus, Mary, and Martha for this festive Seder; and, now if you'll excuse me, I am going to bed. Tomorrow may turn out to be a long day." After clearing the table and washing the dishes, the women followed the example of Jesus and turned in for the night. The men followed suit with the exception of Peter, Judas, and Nathanael who remained at the table to take care of the rest of the wine.

• • •

The Galileans set out for Jerusalem a little before the seventh hour on the fifteenth day of Nisan. When they arrived at the garden of Gethsemane, Jesus called them together as the massive Temple came into view. "Our time has come my loyal and very special friends. Do you have any questions?"

"What if they try to arrest us?" Nathanael asked.

"There will be no resistance," Jesus replied. "We will continue our protest in prison."

"Can we recruit other pilgrims to join us?"

"Absolutely, Mary," Jesus said as he smiled across at his friend from Magdala. "You are so good at that. The more people who join our protest the better."

"It's important for us to explain to the other pilgrims what this is all about," Nathanael said. "The whole point is to proclaim Jesus's message throughout Judea."

"And to feed and house the poor," Judas interjected.

"How long do you think this protest will go on?" James called out from the back of the group.

"Until we have achieved our goals," Jesus responded.

"I like your plan, my good brother."

When no further questions were forthcoming, Jesus bowed his head in prayer. "Yahweh, you informed our people about your desire for economic justice when you gave us the Law. Today we honor that Law. May you be with us as we try to open the eyes of your priests to the needs of your children who are without homes." As Jesus finished his brief petition, he raised his head and smiled deeply as he gazed upon his group of loyal followers. "On to Jerusalem," he called out with enthusiasm. "Just follow behind our dear friend Lazarus."

• • •

As the group of Galileans passed the East Gate of the Temple ten minutes later, nine Roman soldiers, with swords drawn, arrested Jesus. They led him to Golgotha, a bare hill having the form of a skull, which was situated outside of Jerusalem, but quite near the city walls. There they placed him on a cross with ten fellow sufferers, many of whom were already dead.[8]

Notes

1. The ninth day of Nisan falls between late March and early April.
2. See the discussion of Jesus's entry into Jerusalem in the Explanatory Notes.
3. Hosea 6:6.

4. Isaiah 56: 7.

5. See the discussion of the Last Supper in the Explanatory Notes.

6. The celebrant eats the vegetables by dipping them in the salt water, which symbolizes the tears shed by the Israelites during their time of slavery in Egypt.

7. A sweet brown paste of nuts and fruit.

8. For a discussion of the arrest of Jesus see the Explanatory Notes.

## 12: A New Day

The next morning Mary, the mother of Jesus, was desperate to see her son. Mary of Magdala and Sarah wanted to go with her. They talked Lazarus into taking them early as the sun was rising. No one had slept very well. Peter and James came with them. The others were scared or too despondent to move from the protective shelter of Lazarus's home.

It was mostly a silent trip. The exhausted mourners were too numb to speak. They descended slowly down the Mount of Olives, the three women fighting back tears, the three men leading the way with bowed heads. They passed the Temple on their right and then the Tower of Siloam. "I hate this place," James said to no one in particular. "It poisons our religion and takes our money. Now it has taken my brother and our Master," and he collapsed on the ground from the pain of his inconsolable grief. Peter waited patiently for him to regain some measure of composure, helped him to his feet, and placed his arm around him as the two men joined up again with the three women.

They continued walking through the Kidron valley to the south end of Jerusalem. Not twenty minutes after passing the city wall, the hill at Golgotha came into view. There were several Roman soldiers guarding it. The many crosses jumped out at them. Peter counted eleven that were in use. Most of the men on them were dead, their bodies decaying, large chunks of them missing from animals who were left free to devour them. Abandoned skulls and bones were scattered throughout the hill. Mary of Magdala walked off in the distance, and immediately became sick. She never returned that day. She was lost in her sadness and her grief.

Mary, his mother, finally found her son on the left-hand side, naked on a cross, his head sagging, his eyes fixed on the ground. Because of her distance from him, she could not tell if he was still breathing. She fell on her knees, and cursed her God. Eventually James came to her, and led her back home.

Peter took in the scene and fled. Lazarus bid one final farewell to his Master, and took Sarah by the hand to lead her home.[1]

• • •

The Galileans were in no hurry to leave the home of Lazarus and his two sisters. The pain, the disbelief, and the shock of their loss had put them in a state of collective depression, which so drained their energy it was impossible for them to face another four-day journey. They worried some about Mary of Magdala who had not returned from the trip to Golgotha, but the self-absorption from their grief kept them from searching for her.

On the second day of this vigil, Judas could stand it no longer. He had to do something to redeem himself, although no one suspected him for his role in betraying Jesus. He left the home of Lazarus a little after the third hour in search of the killing field called Golgotha. He found it a little before noon.

The scene was grim. In fact, it was disgusting. He too felt sick, and tears filled his eyes as he located his Master on the left edge of the killing field. He was almost certainly dead, Judas concluded, which led him to go immediately to the base of the hill to speak to a Roman soldier. "Kind sir," Judas said. "My Master is dead, and he is a Jew. Can I take him from his cross and bury him?"

"Insurrectionists have no right to be buried. We want you to watch the animals eat him. Maybe then you will think twice about becoming one yourself. Now leave quickly. My comrades will soon join me for a game of cards."

Judas left with a heavy heart and a sagging spirit. Ten minutes into his journey, he yelled out in agony: "My God, my God, why did you desert my Master? Why didn't you intervene to prevent this despicable tragedy? My plan was to force you to intervene to protect my Master, your son." He continued in a halting voice, almost to himself: "My Master was right.

There are no messiahs." Finally, he shouted out once more. "I hate you, Yahweh. My Master was wrong. There is no such thing as a God that loves." He then fell to his knees and cried uncontrollably for the first time in as long as he could remember. When there were no longer tears for him to cry, he got up from the ground and wandered into the city of Jerusalem. He never returned to the home of Lazarus.

The mood in Bethany was much the same. Sapphua and Mary, the sister of Lazarus, prepared an evening meal that was hardly touched. Most spent their time alone or with spouses trying to understand what had happened to them and how they would live the rest of their lives without Jesus.

On the third day following Jesus's death, an amazing change took place. Mary of Magdala came bursting into the house just as the sun was rising. "Our Master is alive," she shouted. "Our Master is alive." Tired eyes looked at her in disbelief. "He is alive in heaven. He spoke to me from there."[2]

"What did he say? Tell us what he said," Sarah asked in an excited voice as she looked up from the dough she was kneading.

"I had this most beautiful vision. He was sitting in heaven. I think God was nearby. He told me I could always love him, that love never dies. He told me he was saving a place for me there. He told me to continue his work of telling Israel about their God of love."

"Are you sure it was our Master?" Peter asked, also in a new voice of excited expectation.

"I felt him. I sensed him all around me. His love filled me. I recognized his voice."

"I believe you, Mary," Nathanael said. "I knew our Master was special; very, very special. We Jews have always believed that God's martyrs were taken to heaven. Now our Master is telling us he is saving a place for us there."

The feeling among the group regarding Mary's revelation and Nathanael's explanation was mixed. Some believed it with an excited joy while others weren't so sure.

The balance shifted when Mary, his mother, entered the courtyard from the barn the next morning. "I saw my son. Mary was right. He sits with God in heaven. He filled my heart with gladness. He was with me all night."

"Did he speak to you like he did to Mary?" Peter asked.

"He did! Yes, he did. I recognized his voice. It was the voice of my son."

"What did he say Mary? Did he give us instructions?"

"Peter, you must have been listening too," Mary said with a loving smile as she looked over at him. "He told us to relocate here, that the kingdom of God would first break out in Jerusalem."

"I can feel his presence all around us," Lazarus chimed in with joy. "This is a new day, a glorious day. You can rebuild your lives here, on our farm, while we work to build God's kingdom in Jerusalem."

"Praise be to God," James said.

"You need to do more than send praise to God, James my son. You better ask for guidance too. He told me in that vision that you are to lead us in Jerusalem."

"That is a burden I do not feel prepared to undertake."

"You have no choice James. The Master has spoken," Peter said as he crossed the room to embrace the new leader of the movement that had so changed the direction of his life.

"Then gather around everybody. We have much work to do. We must gather the people of Israel to hear the message of our glorious God of love. While we await our reunion with our Master in heaven, as Lazarus just suggested, we will work to build God's kingdom in Jerusalem."

Notes

1. For a discussion of the death of Jesus see the Explanatory Notes.
2. For a discussion of the resurrection of Jesus, see the Explanatory Notes.

## Explanatory Notes

*Introduction*

The comments that follow will explain the main assumptions I have made in writing this novel. As I indicated in the Forward, the first big one is that God is love. You discover this God when your heart fills. For me, this happens most frequently when I serve my neighbor, when I reach out to others in kindness.

Why does a full heart point to God? Again for me, I see myself as a biological creature. The parts of my body work according to biological principles. My consciousness is organized around the need for survival. It provides me with a self-centered perspective. I don't find love inside me to change that perspective. Instead love exists outside my body, and enters in when I reach out to others. I don't create the love within me. As Paul points out in Romans 7:18, "nothing good dwells within me." I can only receive it from the outside. For lack of a better word, I call the love I receive, God. The great Jewish theologian Martin Buber led me to this insight.

There is another aspect about love that points to God. The experience of deep love is transforming. It takes you to another place. It fills you with a sense of awe and wonder. When I'm at this "other place," I feel as if I'm in the presence of God. I sense I am grounded in something so much greater than the biological me.

An important corollary comes from this first assumption. I am a Christian because I believe that Jesus, a first century Palestinian Jew, reflects this love in a way few other humans have been able to achieve. This novel paints a picture of what Jesus might have looked like if these assumptions are correct: that God is love and that Jesus reflects that love.

*The Marriage of Jesus*

I hope I caught your attention with the image of Jesus standing naked under a waterfall holding his pregnant wife. You might be surprised to learn that this assumption is historically plausible. It was very unusual for a first century Palestinian man to be single. The vast majority of adult males were married.

This opening to the novel illustrates a problem with the New Testament that few Christians are aware of or are willing to consider. We know next to nothing about the Jesus of history. Historians are confident about only two aspects of Jesus's life: that he was a Jew and that he was crucified by the Romans. Sadly, with these two exceptions, historians have difficulty locating the Jesus of history. Dominique Crossan points out it's like searching for a subatomic particle. You look through the most powerful microscope and find nothing. All you notice is the effect.

What has caused this problem? The most important factor is the first Jewish/Roman war that spanned the years 66 to 73 CE. This war was an earth-shaking event. In 70, Jerusalem was burned and the Temple destroyed. One million Jews were killed as a result of the war according to Josephus, the first century Jewish historian, one hundred thousand Jews were enslaved, and the vast majority of those few who survived, fled. While Josephus's figures probably inflate the number of Jews who died in this war, the picture these figures paint is accurate. The first Jewish/ Roman war was a disaster for Jews living in Palestine.

With regard to the question at hand, most of the historical data pertaining to Jesus was lost or destroyed as a consequence of this war. The gospels of Nazarenes, Hebrews, and Ebionites disappeared. These gospels were written in Palestine where the events took place and were much earlier than the New Testament gospels. We know of them only through the writings of the early church fathers in the second and third century because they refer to these gospels.

An adult male in first century Palestine lived to an average age of thirty-five or forty. Few adult males survived the war. The Christian gospels were written in Greek in the Hellenistic world. What does all this mean? It means that it is extremely unlikely the Christian gospels were written by eyewitnesses to the events. The Jesus movement had to move to the Hellenistic world and become established before gospels were written. That is why the vast majority of scholars date Mark, the first gospel to be written, at 70 CE or later. The crucifixion took place forty years before Mark wrote his gospel. It is highly unlikely eyewitnesses were living forty years after Jesus died with the ability to write in Greek. Remember there was a war, that adult males rarely lived beyond forty, and that Jesus's followers were illiterate peasants.

There is another problem that contributes to this lack of historical data. Ancient historians who wrote about first century Palestine focused their efforts on Judea and more specifically Jerusalem. They wrote about kings, military campaigns, the Temple, and aristocratic court intrigue. They had no interest in writing about Galilean peasants living in tiny villages like Nazareth. We know little about these peasants.

In light of the problem of credible historical information, where did the data for the gospels come from? It came from stories told about Jesus that were passed along orally for forty years. These stories were not originally written down, but passed along by word of mouth. It was a huge telephone game. So much information was unfortunately distorted in this very human process, so much historical data was lost. Interestingly, this data problem is common with ancient biography, and not limited to the Christian gospels.

There is no historical data to suggest Jesus was not married. The New Testament does not provide any evidence one way or the other. The gospels begin their Christian stories with the ministry of Jesus. We know nothing about his first thirty years. Again, the fact that the vast majority of adult males were married in first century Palestine makes it credible to assume Jesus was married too.

In my book on Evangelical Christianity, I argue that Jesus was a first century feminist. This novel helps to explain that. I give him a fantastic wife and a loving mother.

*Cultural Differences Between Galilee and Judea*

The higher status of women in Galilee points to fascinating differences between the two provinces of Galilee and Judea. The starting point for understanding these differences is to examine the history and culture of Judea, home of the southern tribes of Israel, and Galilee where the northern tribes resided. According to Richard Horsley in *Galilee: History, Politics, People* the history and culture of these two provinces in ancient Israel couldn't be more different. The two provinces were united under the reigns of David and Solomon, but following Solomon's death in 931 BCE the northern tribes in Galilee broke away to form their own state. They remained independent until conquered by Assyria in 722 BCE which was followed with domination by Persians, Ptolemies, and Seleucids. Eventually Galilee was conquered by the Hasmoneans, the Judean temple-state, in 104 BCE.

In contrast, the kingdom of Judea remained relatively independent for three hundred years following the death of Solomon until the Egyptians began to exert control in 609 BCE. Judea was conquered by Babylon in 586 BCE which was followed by domination by Persia, Greece, the Seleucid empire, and Rome. As is evident from this history, Galilee and Judea had separate existences for 800 years.

Unlike Judea, the villages of Galilee had no central institution like the Temple to unite them. The Temple in Jerusalem was remote from their lives, a five day walk away, and a source of bitterness because of the taxes imposed during periods of Judean domination. Again, in contrast to Judea, the Galilean tribes lacked a landed aristocracy and sacred scriptures. Galilee was a land of tiny villages and free landowners. An independent spirit developed among the many tiny villages that was fostered by a rugged mountain terrain which made communication and trade difficult. One result of these contrasting histories was different religious traditions.

We assume the coming of a messiah to rescue Israel was a prominent idea held throughout Israel, but it was primarily a Judean hope. David was not a hero for Galileans. Moses was their man. David and Solomon were both resented because of the taxes imposed on Galileans to pay for their wars and building projects.

There is a fascinating debate in 1 Samuel about whether Israel should have a king. In chapter 8 both God and Samuel oppose a king arguing that only Yahweh could be king, a position with wide support in Galilee. In chapter 9 God changes his mind and supports the establishment of a monarchy to protect Israel from the Philistines. See 1 Samuel 9: 16-17 and 10: 24. This second position from 1 Samuel on the monarchy reflects the opinions of the Temple elite in Jerusalem. Jesus's favorite prophet, Isaiah, agreed with the Galileans on the question of a king, arguing that only Yahweh can be king (See Isaiah 43: 15, 44: 6, and 52: 7).

A careful reading of Jesus's teachings on the subject in the Synoptic gospels indicates he was true to his Galilean heritage. According to Luke (4: 43-44), proclaiming the kingdom of God was what Jesus was sent to do. The key passages in the Lord's prayer on the subject (Matthew 6: 9-10) tell us that God will bring in the kingdom. You do not pray for the messiah or the Son of Man to come, but for the kingdom of God to arrive. The parable of the seed growing secretly (Mark 4: 26-29) is about the coming kingdom. Note that no messiah is involved. It's not about liberation, but the mysterious action of God.

In all of Jesus's statements in the four gospels about the coming of God's kingdom, no mention is made of a messiah bringing it in. Many would disagree with this assertion citing the Son of Man references as evidence. A careful comparison of Jesus's statements concerning the coming kingdom and those attributed to the Son of Man indicate that the two sets of statements could not have come from the same person. Jesus calls for a kingdom within history for Israel. The Son of Man passages call for a kingdom in heaven coming at the end of history when the world is destroyed and the righteous lifted up.

These differences between the two cultures are reflected in the novel in several ways. In addition to the higher status of women in Galilee and the idea that God will bring in the kingdom without a messiah, Jesus reflects Galilean ambiguity toward the Temple, and comes out strongly against the sacrifice system. The holiness code was also treated very differently. Galileans paid far less attention to laws regarding purity, dietary regulations, and the sabbath than their Judean counterparts.

*The Pharisees*

Chapter 4 has a scene where Jesus is introduced to the Pharisees in Jerusalem. You will note Jesus does not really differ with them in this scene. In point of fact, it is likely they shared some common values. When you get to Chapter 8, Jesus again comes in contact with the Pharisees, and this time they disagree.

The important point is that all of Jesus's meetings with the Pharisees in the novel take place in Jerusalem, not in Galilee as the New Testament gospels indicate. The Jerusalem setting is historically accurate. Most New Testament scholars argue that, at the time of Jesus, the Pharisees were a small party confined to Jerusalem who were seen as upper-class Temple retainers. They were known as experts in the interpretation of religious law. There is no historical evidence of Pharisees operating in Galilee at the time of Jesus. This would be especially true for tiny villages like Nazareth.

As I indicate above, this is not the view of the New Testament, however. What is going on here? Many New Testament scholars suggest the Pharisees are used as a foil, a device to explain the religion of Jesus by contrasting it with the views of the Pharisees. The gospels exaggerate the differences between them in adopting this strategy. These scholars also assume the stories are invented, which is credible if historians are correct about the Pharisees not venturing into Galilee.

These scholars explain the bitter conflict described in the New Testament between Jesus and the Pharisees in an interesting way. It is a side effect of the Jewish/Roman war. Prior to 70 CE, the Jewish religion was centered around the Temple. When the Temple was destroyed in 70 CE, the central focus shifted to the synagogue where the Pharisees played the dominant role. After 70 CE, the Pharisees became the dominant force in Judaism.

As with Christianity, Judaism reestablished itself in the Hellenistic world after the horror of Rome burning Jerusalem in 70 CE. Christianity during this early period was a Jewish sect. As the Pharisees struggled to preserve Judaism after the war, they came in conflict with these Jewish Christians. This conflict was often bitter. Many scholars argue the conflict between the two groups in the latter half of the first century was added to stories passed down about Jesus from a much earlier period. Again, these scholars assume the conflict stories between Jesus and the Pharisees were largely invented.

But I have strayed a long way from the main point. Historians almost universally agree that the Pharisees during the time of Jesus were confined to Jerusalem. It is almost unthinkable with the primitive communications of the first century that the Pharisees would have had any idea about the activities of a Galilean peasant. Therefore, when I confine the encounters between Jesus and the Pharisees to Jerusalem, I believe I am standing on firm historical ground.

You will note in chapter 9 that Jesus tells a story of two priests coming to Nazareth and condemning Joses and his neighbor Reuben for working on the sabbath. These priests came from Sepphoris and may well have had ties to the Pharisees in Jerusalem. Priests in cities like Sepphoris had to return to Jerusalem to work at the Temple for each of the three main festivals and for two weeks every year to assist with the atonement services where animals were sacrificed. Such priests often shared the values of the Pharisees which is reflected in the novel in the confrontation regarding the sabbath.

*The Birth of Jesus*

The idea that Jesus's father was a Roman general I'm sure got your attention. Let me make a few points in defense of this claim.

The first point to make is that the virgin birth stories in Matthew (1: 18-2:23) and Luke (1:3-2: 39) are fictional stories. This becomes readily apparent when the two stories are compared. You need to make this comparison yourself by listing the events in the two stories in order to fully grasp the idea that fictional stories exist in the New Testament. When I make such a study, here is what I find.

In Matthew, the story begins with Mary and Joseph residing in Bethlehem. We quickly learn that Mary is with child as a result of some mysterious intervention by the Holy Spirit. Jesus is born in Bethlehem and visited by wise men. Because it was believed that a king of the Jews had been born, the current king, Herod, is threatened. He instructs the wise men to go to Bethlehem to locate Jesus, and then to report back to him so he can pay his respects too. The wise men find Jesus by following a star, which seems to wander around in the universe. While with the family, the wise men offer gifts and have a dream telling them to return home a different way so as to avoid reporting to Herod. Soon after they leave, Joseph has a dream telling him to escape to Egypt with Mary and Jesus. In anger and frustration for being duped, Herod kills all male children in the surrounding area under two years of age. When Herod dies, an angel again appears to Joseph, informing him it is now safe to leave Egypt. The family relocates to Nazareth.

In Luke, the story begins with Zechariah and Elizabeth, the parents of John the Baptist. Elizabeth conceives John the Baptist as a result of a miracle. In this case, God solves a fertility problem. The Angel Gabriel explains to Mary that she will also have a child, conceived by the Holy Spirit. Mary visits her cousin Elizabeth. She sings the Magnificat, and John is born. The story now moves to the birth of Jesus in earnest. Caesar Augustus orders a census, which causes Mary and Joseph to make the trip from Nazareth to Bethlehem. Note that they reside in Nazareth. Mary gives birth at an inn in Bethlehem witnessed by shepherds. Jesus is circumcised at the Temple, and the family returns to Nazareth.

Most Christians do not make such an outline when considering these stories. Instead they conflate elements from both stories, and this composite picture is reinforced every Christmas when the Christmas pageant is performed in their church. However, if you are honest and objective in your examination of the two stories, it jumps out at you that the stories have nothing in common. One is the story of the birth of a king with a star wandering around the universe, wise men visiting, children dying, and a trip to Egypt. The story in Luke is about the birth of a Palestinian peasant in a simple inn with shepherds in attendance and a quick return to Nazareth.

There is only one possible conclusion from this summary. One of these stories is fiction. They cannot both be true. This is an important insight because it demonstrates that fictional accounts do in fact occur in the New Testament. In fact, both stories are fiction. Why? To begin with, Paul never mentions a virgin birth in any of his letters. Paul is one of the greatest salesmen in history. If a virgin birth happened, he would have proclaimed it in every letter he wrote. Instead, Paul hints in both Romans (1:3-4) and Galatians (4: 4) that the birth of Jesus occurred through normal human processes.

Mark never mentions a virgin birth. John also fails to mention it. The author of John suggests in chapter 6 that Jesus was born through normal human processes. In chapter 1, he indicates that Jesus was born in Nazareth (1: 45-56. See also John 7:42). The Virgin Birth of Jesus is nowhere mentioned in a history of the period nor in any other New Testament document. Think about the claim, virgin birth. It's an amazing one with no independent historical confirmation. In all of world literature, the claim is made only in Matthew and Luke.

There are also historical problems with the two stories. The census mentioned in Luke never took place. The evangelist uses it as a device to get Mary to Bethlehem so that the birth will confirm the prophecy of Micah (5:2)—an example of prophecy creating history. The evangelist created a story to prove Micah's prophecy. To repeat, the worldwide census never took place. There was a smaller one in Syria, however, when Jesus was ten.

Can you imagine a nine-month pregnant woman walking five or six days to get to Bethlehem? How about the star that wanders around the universe or the wise men who make a long journey to honor the birth of a Galilean peasant? These elements of Matthew's story stretch the imagination.

Bethlehem was seven miles from Jerusalem, the home of Herod. Why did Herod have to ask wise men for help in locating Jesus? And then there's the killing of all those children. History reports that Herod killed a few of his own kids, but there is no record of an atrocity like the one described by Matthew.

Finally, stories of miraculous births were common in ancient literature for great men. Such stories were written for Moses, Samuel, John the Baptist, Apollonius of Tyana, Alexander the Great, Romulus, Augustus Caesar to name a few. Do we believe those stories?

As I point out in the discussion of Jesus's marriage, we know nothing about the first thirty years of his life. We can now add to that list the birth of Jesus with one exception. The Mishnah, a collection of Jewish oral traditions dating from the third century CE, makes reference to Pantera, a Roman general as the father of Jesus. Although we do not know the precise date when Jesus was born, it is quite likely he was born during the occupation of Nazareth by the Roman army in their siege of Sepphoris in 4 BCE.

This is the only hint we have outside of the fictional stories in the New Testament regarding the birth of Jesus; and it is, admittedly, slim evidence. So why include it? I included it in the story because I wanted to emphasize again and again the consequences of relating to a God of love. Such a God is inclusive. Her deep love is equally available for all to receive. This God of love would never create laws that discriminated against people due to accidents of birth.

*The Family of Jesus*

In the novel, I depict the family of Jesus providing enthusiastic support for his work. This is not the view of the New Testament. In Mark 3: 20-21, Jesus's family pronounces him to be crazy. A little later on (Mark 6: 1-6) Jesus is rejected by all the members of his family. It is interesting that despite these claims James, the brother of Jesus, leads the Christian community in Jerusalem after the crucifixion (Acts 15:13-21 and Acts 21: 19). In addition, Jesus's mother and brothers are prominent members of that first congregation. (Acts 1:14)

Luke adds to Mark's story of Jesus's rejection by his family (4: 16-30). In Luke's version, Jesus reads from a scroll at the synagogue. Nazareth was a village of maybe one hundred peasant families. It is very unlikely such a poor community could afford a scroll. While it is true I have Jesus read from a scroll in Capernaum, Capernaum was a much larger village. It was also a fishing community, which provided its residents with a higher standard of living.

At the end of Jesus's performance in Luke's version of the story, the crowd is so angry they attempt to throw Jesus off a cliff. While Nazareth is nestled on the side of a mountain, researchers have searched in vain for a suitable cliff to throw someone from. In a tiny place like Nazareth, it is difficult to imagine the existence of a crowd. These problems lead some scholars to conclude the author of Luke knew nothing about Nazareth or Jesus's family, and so he invented the story.

Jesus was known as a loving man, a charismatic speaker, and a doer of remarkable deeds. I can't believe he would not have had the enthusiastic support of his family. The problems discussed above lend credibility to my position.

Finally, I cannot believe Jesus would encourage his followers to leave their families in order to follow him. To leave your family under such circumstances is a profoundly selfish act. If the person leaving is the breadwinner, this selfish action could lead to the starvation of his family. For a man who preached serving your neighbor, such a teaching to encourage your followers to leave their families is hypocrisy.

*The Death of John the Baptist*

According to Matthew (14:3-12) and Mark (6:17-29), Herod puts John in prison for criticizing him for marrying his brother's wife Heriodias. John was then beheaded because the daughter of Heriodias so beguiled Herod at his birthday party he promised her anything she wanted. She chooses the head of John the Baptist which Herod gives her. Luke truncates the story (3: 19-20), and the gospel of John omits it entirely. I guess the writer of John was not into reporting soap opera-like events.

Josephus, the first century Jewish historian, reports that Herod executed John because he saw him as a political threat. Josephus's version of the story makes much more sense to me. It is the one I have used in the novel.

On another matter, you have probably noticed my treatment of John the Baptist differs greatly from the material in the New Testament. The gospels portray John as the forerunner of Jesus. The writer of the gospel of John even hints that Jesus may have begun his career as a disciple of John. In addition, the gospels all contain self-deprecating statements from John: that he is not worthy to stoop down and untie Jesus's shoes, that he baptizes with water while Jesus baptizes with the Holy Spirit.

Josephus in writing his histories of first century Palestine pays more attention to John the Baptist than to Jesus. There may even have been some competition between the two movements. I see the John the Baptist material in the gospels as invented by the evangelists to enhance the reputation of Jesus at the expense of John. While I'm convinced John's message is accurately portrayed in the gospels, I am also convinced that a loving Jesus would find it distasteful.

*The Miracles*

As you have probably noticed, the miraculous elements are missing from my discussion of what the Jewish historian Josephus described as "the great deeds" of Jesus. Dominic Crossan makes a distinction between curing disease and healing disease. My son the doctor cures disease. He attacks the biological causes of the problem. In my novel, Jesus heals disease by making people feel better about themselves. The mind, as medical science freely admits, is a powerful tool in healing disease.

Most Christians don't like Crossan's distinction. They see Jesus as more able to cure disease than my son. It's two thousand years too late to set up a contest between the two, but Christians who believe literally in Jesus's miracles need to take into consideration several historical problems with the miracle stories.

In the first place, the understanding of disease in first century Palestine was different from what it is today. Disease was not caused by biological processes in the body breaking down, but by Satan. Disease occurred when evil forces invaded the body. When Jesus healed disease, he was battling Satan. It was war. This view is consistent throughout the New Testament. See Mark 3: 11-12. In addition, you can read the miracle stories in Luke, chapters 4-8, to get a sense of this different worldview.

The nature miracles where Jesus walks on water, feeds the 5,000, and calms the storm imply a similar worldview. The universe according to ancient belief was not governed by the laws of nature. Instead God was in control. God maintained order out of chaos. He intervened directly in the natural order to achieve his will. Does this type of intervention continue to happen or is such a belief unique to the ancient world? If God can feed a hungry 5,000, why doesn't he intervene to feed a hungry modern world? To believe in the nature miracles, you must deny the claims of modern science that the universe is governed by natural laws. I am not willing to do that.

Returning to disease, if you believe Jesus cured it, what about all the other magical healers in first century Palestine? There was Honi the Circle-Drawer, a first century Galilean, Rabbi Hanina ben Dosa who lived near Nazareth, and Apollonius of Tyana who not only was known for his miraculous cures; but he was also believed to have been born as a result of divine intervention and to have ascended to heaven after his death. In addition, we have Eleazar the Essene and Rabbi Simon ben Yohai, both of whom were known for casting out demons. And don't forget Elijah and Elisha of Old Testament fame. The gospel writers patterned many of Jesus's miracles after similar ones performed by them. Finally, in Acts, Paul heals many victims of disease and raises a person to life. The disciples heal the sick and cast out demons.

Do we believe the stories about these men? The stories are remarkably similar to those told about Jesus. Read the story about Jesus and Beelzebul in Matthew 12: 22-24. In the story, Jesus cures a blind and dumb demoniac. The Pharisees don't question Jesus's ability to cure disease. Religious leaders were expected to perform such feats in first century Palestine. Their only question was where did his power come from. They believe the devil in the case of Jesus.

Then there are the technical problems with the stories. The disease is never accurately diagnosed. Are we sure the man had leprosy? We never know whether the cure lasts. Remarkable claims require solid historical evidence to be believable—at least for me. It is also interesting that almost without exception a miracle story is told to make a theological point.

Take the story of the resurrection of Lazarus in John 11: 1-44 as an example. The purpose of the story is as much to support the concept of realized eschatology, the idea that the kingdom is now, a matter of the heart, than to amaze people with Jesus's miraculous powers. When Jesus tells Martha that Lazarus will rise again, she thinks of the common expectation that he will rise in the future after God judges the world. Jesus corrects her by saying the kingdom is now, that anyone who believes in him will have life now. One suspects the writer, at least in part, created this story to make this theological point.

It is interesting that the story of bringing back Lazarus to life is only told in the gospel of John. And yet it is the most dramatic miracle in the New Testament. Jesus states clearly that Lazarus is dead, and he does not come to Bethany until Lazarus has been dead in his tomb for four days. Jesus does not want people to think Lazarus was merely asleep. You would think if eyewitnesses wrote these accounts and if the miracle actually occurred, this remarkable story would have been in every gospel.

I include the Lazarus story in my novel, however, for personal reasons. I once healed my grandmother in much the same way Lazarus is healed in my novel. My wife Lyn and I were living with our infant daughter Heather in New Orleans where I was attending Tulane as a graduate student. One night I received a call from my uncle saying his mother, my grandmother, was not doing well and could we visit. I said sure. I was writing a dissertation that could wait.

When we arrived at her home in Florida, we learned she was in the hospital with the scary prognosis she would not survive the night. I went immediately to her room and found her in a coma. I did not know what to say to God in prayer, so I held her hand throughout a long night.

After three or four hours, the nurse came in and said: "You know, her blood pressure is a little better." She left, and I kept holding my grandmother's hand. She awoke the next morning around 10 am., confused. She wondered where her son had gone. She had wanted to say goodbye to him. She thought it was my uncle who had spent the night holding her hand. She lived for three more years. The mind is a powerful tool for healing.

Dealing with the miracle stories was the most difficult challenge I faced in writing the novel. The fact that Jesus had a reputation as a miracle worker is well supported within the historical tradition. The gospels attest to this fact as does Josephus, the first century Jewish historian who was not a believer. On the other hand, there were all the problems I describe above. There is no evidence for God intervening to alter the natural order of things in the twenty-first century. The holocaust was the tipping point for me. No God of love who intervened in the natural order would have allowed that to happen. The fact that God would make an exception for first century Palestine does not make sense.

My problem was that I could not imagine what Jesus or all the other miracle workers I list above for the first century did to create the impression that a miraculous healing had taken place. As a result, Jesus heals a leper in the novel by examining the face of a sufferer and concluding there was no evidence for the disease. He casts out demons by making victims feel better about themselves. He feeds crowds of people by asking them to share with others the food they had brought for the occasion. I have his followers talk about miracles he performed in places the novel does not directly visit. This approach will probably leave many readers disappointed; but, sadly, it is the best I could do.

*The Kingdom of God*

The kingdom of God is a slippery concept in the New Testament. There are three different views as to what it means, and these different concepts often exist alongside each other in the gospel writings.

There is the traditional Jewish view of a kingdom on earth ruled by God or God's agent. There is important evidence in the gospels that Jesus talks about such a kingdom. A good example is found in Matthew 16:17 and Luke 22: 28-30 where Jesus promises the disciples, because of their loyalty, that each one would sit on a throne to judge a tribe of Israel. In Mark 14: 25, Jesus speaks of eating and drinking in the kingdom. According to Luke (13: 23-29), people from all corners of the earth will come to take their place in the kingdom, but the unrighteous will be cast aside.

A second view posits a kingdom in heaven for the righteous. A time of cosmic judgment will arrive. Most humans won't make it. They will burn, be destroyed. However, the righteous followers of Jesus will be saved. The Son of Man will swoop down from the clouds of heaven to rescue the righteous and bring them to heaven. See Mark 14: 62. Although Paul never mentions the Son of Man in his letters, he has a similar view (see 1 Thessalonians 4: 16-18).

This is the most prevalent view in the New Testament. It was clearly the position of the early church. Whether it was Jesus's view is debatable. Norman Perrin, in his book *Rediscovering the Teaching of Jesus*, makes a fascinating point related to this issue. He argues the most authentic statement of Jesus's message comes from the parables. These stories are highly original, contain Aramaic idioms, and reflect Palestinian culture and peasant life. Almost without exception, the message of the parables is about the coming of God's kingdom to the land of Israel.

In contrast, the early church interprets the resurrection of Jesus in terms of the Son of Man teachings in Daniel 7: 13. Jesus is seen as a transcendent, pre-existent, heavenly being who will judge the world in a cataclysmic event at the end of time. When this event takes place, the righteous will be rewarded with eternal life in heaven and sinners will be left on earth to burn. Many of these Son of Man statements come from the lips of Jesus. This Son of Man image is an important one in the New Testament. It is far and away the most common image used to describe Jesus.

Perrin's point is that these two ideas of the kingdom could not come from the same person. Jesus preached about a future kingdom on earth which God would establish. The church preached about the return of Jesus as the Son of Man and a future kingdom in heaven. Jesus prayed in the Lord's Prayer for God's kingdom to come. The church prayed for Jesus as the Son of Man to come. What is amazing is the liberties taken by the church in placing this message on the lips of Jesus.

As I point out above, we know the early church possessed these apocalyptic views of Jesus's role in establishing God's kingdom in heaven, but that does not mean that these views go back to the historical Jesus. I reject this second view of the kingdom because it assumes the judgment of a mean-spirited God bent on revenge. Apocalyptic visions are all about getting even with your enemies. I can't imagine a God of love acting in that way.

The third view of the kingdom is an interesting one. The kingdom is now, a present reality. It exists in communities that are built around love. It is an experiential kingdom located in one's heart.

This view developed later among certain Christians when it became clear to them the expectation of an imminent judgment and establishment of a kingdom by divine intervention was not happening any time soon. It had not happened as most Jews and Jewish Christians had expected. You see hints of this third position in Luke 17: 20-21. The concept is more fully developed in the gospel of John. See John chapter 4 verses 14, 23 and 36 and John 11: 21-26.

As you have noticed from reading the novel, this is the kingdom

I see Jesus establishing. While the other two views have many scholarly proponents, the second one in particular violates my central assumption about religion that God is love. I just can't imagine a loving Jesus advancing the idea of a kingdom predicated on the need for judgment by a petty, nasty, revenge driven God. I am indebted to John Dominic Crossan for the idea of the kingdom being one of radical love and equality that one works to build on earth.

*Jesus's Entry into Jerusalem*

I avoid this story. Read about it in Matthew 21: 1-11. In Matthew's story, the author relates that Jesus tells the disciples to find a colt and a donkey for him to ride into Jerusalem. On that trip, we are led to imagine that Jesus straddles both animals as a large crowd of people spreads branches and cloaks along the road proclaiming him king of Israel. Matthew writes the story because it fulfills prophecy from Zechariah (see chapter 9 in Zechariah).

The story has several historical problems aside from the rather comical image of Jesus straddling the two animals. First, it is well known that Jesus confined his ministry to small villages in Galilee. According to Matthew, this was his first trip to Jerusalem. What is difficult to understand is why there would be crowds of people proclaiming this unknown peasant from Galilee as their king.

It is also difficult to understand why the crowd would proclaim him king based on the message of Jesus. His message was about the coming of God's kingdom. He never suggested he would be king or that God would appoint a king to take on Rome. Rather it was always clear that God would rule.

Finally, and most important, it is strange that Rome allows this enthusiastic demonstration to take place. Roman soldiers were specifically sent to Jerusalem at Passover to deal with threats of this kind. It was a tense time for Rome. The people of Israel were celebrating their liberation from Egypt. Many Jews expected God to intervene in a similar way to throw out Rome. For crowds of people to proclaim Jesus as king, was a dangerous act, which most likely would have led to Jesus's immediate arrest. Instead Jesus continues to teach at the Temple for another week according to Matthew. Highly improbable!

*The Last Supper*

You may have wondered why there was no portrayal of the Last Supper as a service of Holy Communion in the novel. Such a service came from the imagination of Paul and not from the historical Jesus. It was based on Paul's understanding of Jesus's death on the cross as an atoning sacrifice. No Palestinian Jew would ask his followers to drink his blood, even as a symbolic act. Blood was seen as a foundation block of life, and thus it belonged to God. To drink blood was an act of blasphemy. It was strictly forbidden. We need to always keep in mind that Jesus was a Jew, not the first Christian. Finally, it is amazing to me that so many Christians see Jesus's death on the cross as an atoning sacrifice when his last and most dramatic act is to attack the sacrifice system at the Temple.

In the novel, Jesus shares many common meals with his friends. This tradition has solid support in the New Testament.

*Jesus's Trials before the Sanhedrin and Pilate*

I also omit the story of these two trials because of historical problems. With regard to Jesus's trial before the Sanhedrin, there were no eyewitnesses present to report the proceedings. He appeared before the assembled chief priests and elders alone (Mark 14: 53-54). Where did this story come from? The members of the Sanhedrin certainly would not have provided details of their meeting with Jesus. The disciples fled from Jerusalem. In addition, Jewish Law forbid the Sanhedrin to meet when a major festival event was taking place. It also did not meet at night. Jesus's trial there violated both of these laws. As a result of these problems, it is safe to assume that the story came from the imagination of Mark, the author of the passion narrative whose version of the story was used by Matthew and Luke when creating their stories of Jesus's passion. The gospel of John omits this trial.

The story of Jesus's appearance before Pilate is silly. The story suggests that Pilate sees Jesus as innocent and wants to let him go. He is concerned that an injustice might be committed. This is the man who five years later was fired from his position as prefect of Judea for excessive cruelty. Pilate had no interest in justice, only political order. At the end of the trial, Pilate allows the crowd to decide. He offers to free one prisoner during the festival period, a gift he performed each year at Passover. The problem with this claim is that historians have never found evidence that a Jewish prisoner was pardoned during Passover, either before Jesus's crucifixion or after.

As I indicate above, Pilate leaves it up to the crowd to decide. Their choice is Jesus or Barabbas. The crowd loudly demands that Pilate free Barabbas. It is interesting that the crowd has changed its tune. A week after proclaiming Jesus king, they now want him crucified.

Such trials were not necessary and were not held. The Roman military had the authority and the power to deal with political dissidents. If trials were held for political dissidents and troublemakers, a court would have been in session on a permanent basis with long delays because there were so many political dissidents to try. Instead Rome simply arrested political troublemakers and placed them on a cross. My novel paints such a picture.

*The Death of Jesus*

If this novel becomes a movie, regulators will have to forbid young children from seeing it because of the scene depicting Jesus's death on the cross. It is horrifying. The thought of animals devouring the body of this beautiful man is extremely disturbing. But it happened. The accounts in the New Testament gospels all have significant historical problems.

Crucifixion was a Roman punishment. It was used to get rid of political troublemakers. Historians know a lot about these crucifixions because they were so frequently carried out. The number of political dissenters crucified in the Roman Empire numbered in the ten of thousands.

The first thing about them was there was no trial as I point out above. A second important factor to consider is that burial of victims was not allowed. It was official Roman policy to forbid such burials. The point of crucifixion was for people to watch bodies being devoured. This disgusting spectacle was seen as a deterrent for potential, future political dissenters.

Thousands of Jewish dissidents were crucified during the long period of Roman colonial rule. Archaeologists have exhumed hundreds of Jewish graves throughout the Holy Land in recent years. It is interesting that they have found only one body where the remains suggest crucifixion. Crucified victims were not buried.

*The Resurrection of Jesus*

It is obvious if you have read Chapter 12 that my view of the resurrection is not the traditional one. I see it as a vision experience. This view of the resurrection is historically credible for three important reasons.

The first reason is that the stories of Jesus's physical resurrection in the four gospels are weak. Several points need to be made here. The first is the stories differ in many important ways. Let's examine two major ones. There are many smaller discrepancies you can read about in scholarly treatments of this issue.

The first point is the gospels differ as to where the encounter between Jesus and his disciples takes place. Matthew places the meeting on a mountain in Galilee (28: 16-20) while Luke has this meeting in a house in Jerusalem (24: 33-37). Can you imagine eyewitnesses making that mistake? We are talking about the most amazing event ever alleged to have taken place in human history.

A second major discrepancy is found in the gospel of Matthew. According to Matthew, as Jesus dies on the cross, bodies of Jewish holy men rise from their graves, and walk around Jerusalem. These resurrected holy men appear to many people. (27:51-54) This account is only found in Matthew. Again, can you imagine eyewitnesses or historians for that matter, missing this amazing event?

I cannot. However, it is interesting that historians living in Palestine around the time of Jesus somehow missed several events relating to Jesus's physical resurrection. The only reports of the resurrection appear in the Christian gospels. For some reason, historians of the period missed hearing about these resurrected Jewish leaders. They also missed the earthquake, the eclipse of the sun, and the tearing of the veil protecting the Holy of

Holies at the Temple. All three of these events allegedly occurred as Jesus was dying on the cross according to the gospels.

For me, however, the second and most important problem with these stories is the very small group of people who were privileged to encounter the resurrected Jesus. Jesus appeared physically to the disciples and a few women. That's it. What's at stake is human salvation, a gift granted to those who confess Jesus as their savior according to traditional Christian belief. These stories make Christianity into an exclusive club because the vast majority of Jews living in Jerusalem at the time of the resurrection are prevented from experiencing this great event. This omission makes it less likely for them to confess Jesus as their savior. Can you imagine a God of love limiting salvation to such a small group of people? I cannot. He would have had the resurrected Jesus shake hands with every resident in Jerusalem. However, in the New Testament accounts, nobody but this exclusive group is greeted by Jesus. In Acts (10:41), Peter specifically states that it was God's intention for the resurrected Jesus to meet with only a small, select group of Jesus's closest followers.

The third reason for rejecting the physical resurrection of Jesus is that Paul does. On the Damascus Road, Paul sees Jesus in heaven. It's a vision experience. Jesus is not physically around. He is in heaven sitting at the right hand of God. Read Paul's account of his resurrection encounter with Jesus in Acts 9: 1-9 and Acts 29: 12-17. In Acts 26: 17, Paul specifically states his resurrection experience came as a vision. In 11 Corinthians 12:1-7, Paul talks about his visionary trip to heaven. In 1 Corinthians 15: 3-8, Paul insists his experience was the same as the experiences of the disciples. Please read this last sentence one more time.

Paul was not being naïve in making this assertion. He says in Galatians that very soon after his Damascus experience he met with James, the brother of Jesus, and Peter for fifteen days in Jerusalem. Acts supports this claim. Paul must have discussed the resurrection with them. If Jesus had physically risen from the dead as the four gospels claim before ascending to heaven, Paul would have certainly described it that way.

It is important to remember that Paul was the first person to write about the resurrection of Jesus. Stories about his physical resurrection came later. It is also important to remember that, almost certainly, Jesus's physical body was devoured by animals, making the physical resurrection of his body even more difficult to conceive.

As I'm sure you have noticed, my treatment of the resurrection accepts the traditional view that a new understanding of Jesus came on the third day. In point of fact, this new understanding may have taken a lot longer to achieve; however, with the exception of the time frame, I am comfortable with my assumption that the resurrection of Jesus was a vision experience. Rather than returning physically on the third day, Jesus encountered his close followers from heaven in dreams or vision experiences. Over time these followers came to see him not as the expected messiah, but as the Son of Man. Stephen, the first Christian martyr, makes such a confession just before he is stoned to death on orders of the Sanhedrin. (See Acts 7:56) The idea of the resurrected Jesus as the Son of Man, the preexistent cosmic judge who will return to earth to rescue the righteous and take them to heaven, comes from the early church.

One's view of the resurrection of Jesus has important consequences for the type of religion one affirms. The physical resurrection of Jesus is seen by many Christians as the greatest miracle. It is an event you believe in. Belief in its occurrence becomes a litmus test for Christian membership. It reinforces a religion that centers around belief. One is saved by belief in Jesus Christ as your savior. Why does Jesus have the ability to take one to heaven? The answer is simple: because God physically raised him from the dead. The problem with a religion of belief is that it doesn't change you. It doesn't make you into a new person.

Only an encounter of deep love can do that. The resurrection when understood as a vision experience is about encountering deep love. Revisit Paul's encounter with the resurrected Jesus on the Damascus road. (Acts 9: 1-9) The beautiful thing about love is that it doesn't die. We can experience the death of Jesus in the same way as his original followers when we reflect on and relive the events of his life, when we allow the Jesus story to become an important focus of our life. The point of this novel is to portray the Jesus story in a way that is transforming. To see and experience what he did, what he said, and how he lived can take you to a different place. As I request in the Foreword, please email me at rherrick86@gmail.com to let me know how I did.

READING GUIDE

1.Read the Explanatory Notes regarding the marriage of Jesus. Do the notes make sense or are you still bothered by the idea of a married Jesus?

2. There are many hints in the first two chapters on the economic status of Jesus and his family. Gather that evidence and create a picture of the economic position of Jesus and his family in Galilean society in the first century.

3. In chapter three Jesus asks some very hard questions of his God. What does he conclude?

4. Compare the treatment of John the Baptist in chapter three with the picture of John the Baptist in the New Testament. You may want to consult the Explanatory Notes in undertaking this task. What do you think?

5. In chapter four a central theme of the novel is introduced. Jesus is exposed to the Jewish sacrificial system at the Temple, which he comes to reject. God is about "steadfast love, not sacrifice." (Hosea 6:6) The novel goes on to reject the idea of Jesus as an atoning sacrifice on the cross. What do you think?

6. In chapter four we learn that Jesus's father was a Roman soldier. Read the Explanatory Notes regarding this claim. Are they convincing? Does it matter who his father was?

7. Conservative Christians believe in the rapture, a time when Jesus will return and gather the righteous to take to heaven. The vast majority of us

will be left on earth to burn. The Jesus in the novel rejects such an idea, claiming that a God of love would never use cruel means to achieve such an end. What do you think?

8. In chapter five, Rachel asks Jesus to explain how a God of love can allow Anna to die and she to live as a whore. Comment on his answer.

9. The novel changes Jesus's central mission. In the New Testament, Jesus's mission is to proclaim the imminent coming of God's kingdom in heaven. In the novel, his central mission is to proclaim a God of love. What do you think?

10. In chapter six, Jesus heals a leper. In chapter eight, Jesus brings Lazarus back to life. Read the Explanatory Notes on the miracles. Are they convincing?

11. Jesus commiserates with both Rachel and Mary from Magdala over their divorces. Where does Jesus come from on the issue of divorce?

12. When Jesus addresses the synagogue in Capernaum in chapter six, he speaks about nonviolence. Explain his thinking on this issue.

13. Why will the poor be the first to experience the kingdom of God? What kind of a kingdom is Jesus talking about in the novel? In coming up with your answer, you might want to consult the Explanatory Notes on these questions.

14. Judaism, as a religion in first century Palestine, was centered in the Temple. How in the novel does Jesus change all that?

15. Why is the parable of the Good Samaritan such a powerful tale?

16. Jesus's friends struggle with the question of his identity. Why is this question such a difficult puzzle to solve? Who do you think he is? Has the novel changed your view on the identity of Jesus?

17. Compare the events of the Passion Narrative as they appear in the New Testament with the account given in the novel. After reading the Explanatory Notes, has your view of these events changed?

18. Compare the depiction of the resurrection in the New Testament gospels with the account given in the novel. Again, after reading the Explanatory Notes, has your view of the resurrection changed?

Lightning Source UK Ltd.
Milton Keynes UK
UKHW010726270223
417728UK00004B/359